THE EXTRAVAGANZA ETERNIA

KRISTIN OSANI

THE EXTRAVAGANZA ETERNIA

For my family, chosen and found.

ONE

Leathan should've known that mystic was scamming her when he promised it'd be easy to break her curse.

The thought pinballs around her head as she sequesters herself in an empty corner of the big top backstage, as far from the other troupers as she can get. Chest heaving from her cross-city dash to the circus, eyes burning from sweat and tears she refuses to shed, she digs into her skirt pocket for her compact. She should've known. She *had* known, but she'd ignored the instinct, as she always ignores instincts that spring from the part of her life before she was cursed; a part she can't—won't—remember.

"Thank fuck." Renni's tenor trill cuts through the melange of orchestral music, laughter, and frenetic chatter. The star of the Extravaganza Eternia billows towards her, resplendent in aurora borealis swirls. Shimmer powder dusts his dark calla lily skin; his flowing midnight locs are wrapped in ribbons and crowned in thin silver moonbeams. Leathan's ragged heart leaps at the sight of him, but she shoves it back down for its own protection. "You're here."

"I'm here every night." She keeps her voice neutral. Not too sardonic, not too casual; it could be a statement of fact, or a joke. Whatever Renni wants to read into it.

"You never cut it this close to curtain." There's no anger or accusation in his tone. Only concern, which is worse. Leathan reminds herself Renni shows concern for every trouper in the Extravaganza regardless of the nature of their connection—or lack thereof; that he takes his responsibility for their well-being too seriously. "What happened?"

"Nothing." Avoiding the worry creasing his brown eyes, Leathan flips her compact open, angling the pearlescent clamshell so he can't see she only has enough lihilim power left to weave a single costume change. Static electricity curls up her nose, notes of vanilla and petrichor tingling through her body. "Showtime."

Kaleidoscopic sparkles surround her in a vortex of shooting stars, turn her this way and that, dissolving her street clothes into a curve-hugging riot of curlicuing pastels, mottling her white skin with blue and bronze pigment, weaving verdant leaves and flowers into the braided nest of her auburn hair.

"Nothing my perfect ass." Undeterred, Renni sulks one large shoulder against a steel support beam and squints against the spell light. "Were you trying to break out? You found some mystic who promised to help, but kept stalling and taking more and more magic—"

"No." The lie comes easy to her thin lips, gnawed raw and chapped.

"We all try at least once. Hells, I tried like five times. No one wants to believe it's not possible."

"I lost track of time sightseeing, all right?" Her change complete, she strides to the wings. One minute warnings strobe silent and acrid above troupers scurrying into place.

Renni sidesteps in front of Leathan so quickly she treads on his bare toes. The mostly apologetic, partly irritated profanity on the tip of her tongue shrivels when he whispers, "You're still wearing your pendant."

"I'm not," she rasps, but her hands fly to her chest, where the low V of her costume leaves, dangling in plain view, the pendant that confines her curse.

Hot, visceral horror pulses through her. Lightheaded, she clutches the marble of gold filigreed glass between clammy palms, concealing the desiccated tumbleweed clippings trapped inside, but it's too late.

Renni saw.

"I didn't see," he insists, gaze pointedly on the rafters thirty feet overhead. "Just the light glinting off the chain. I swear."

"I put it away." Sure this is some sort of hiccup in reality, Leathan casts her spiraling mind back for proof, retraces her steps from the moment she took her pendant out of its velvet-lined jewel box in the storage shed. If it were up to her she'd never have to touch the thing, but troupers are contractually forbidden beyond circus bounds without them—so like some morbid little hall pass, around her neck and under her shirt it went.

There it stayed as she arrived at the mystic's tiny parlor, eager and early; as she killed time perusing the capsule machines outside his door until he beckoned her in; as her excitement rotted each time he swore he was close, he just needed one more pinch of magic; as she refused to admit she was being scammed until he drained her compact to a single drop.

And as, in her all-consuming desperation to make the evening show on time—a show she thought she'd never perform in again, a show she'd lose her contract for missing—she sprinted straight to the big top without so much as a glance to the shed.

Leathan coils to dash out the door; but the orchestra lulls, the audience hushes, and their ringmaster's velvet voice rumbles through the big top:

"Fine folk and gentle guests, welcome to Y. Okuiv's Extravaganza Eternia. Please take these last few minutes before the show to silence your devices—"

A high-pitched buzzing in Leathan's ears blanks out the rest of Yokuiv's preamble. Even if she had magic to help her, there's no time to get to the shed. Nowhere nearby to stash her pendant safe and out of sight. No option except to perform with it on, which isn't a fucking option at all. She'd be exposing more of herself than striding out on stage naked. The mere thought of letting herself be seen like that, a dangerous intimacy beyond anything she's let herself have in twenty years, locks her joints in place.

She can't—won't—do it.

Which means she's not performing. Which means she's about to get her third and final strike against the contract binding her to Yokuiv's circus and protection.

The irony isn't lost on her. That trying to break her curse is the reason she's about to be at its mercy again. Not that it'll have much mercy once it's free of its prison. She can already feel it happening: the wind raging around her, flaying her flesh into brittle twigs, breaking her bones into jagged thorns and drying her blood into sticky sap; crushing her into a grotesque tumbleweed to snatch up and tear away from everyone and everything she knows and loves—

"Leathan, breathe." Renni kneels. She doesn't know when she crouched down and clutched her knees to her chest, forcing herself into a tiny ball like it won't hurt so much when her curse takes her if she starts the process herself. Maybe this time it won't. She's been careful, after all, so careful not to form connections with the other troupers. No friends, no lovers, not a single acquaintance. "Breathe. It's all right."

"I have to go," she keens. A trouper struck out years before Leathan was recruited, but the others still gossip in hushed, terrified tones about what happened. If her curse is about to come raging out of its pendant prison with ten years of pent-up wrath to exact on anything in its path, she can't be here. She can't endanger the troupers or the spectators in the stands. She needs to run, summon their ringmaster— only lihilim are powerful enough to neutralize a rogue curse. "I have to get Yokuiv."

"No." Renni clutches her arm as she rises on wobbling legs to flee. "No. I'm not letting that happen again."

The static electricity of Extravaganza magic dances across Leathan's skin. Soft fabric tickles her forehead. Still not looking at her, Renni holds out a fringed kerchief that matches her costume. It crackles with a protective charm he's woven into it.

"Take it." He mimes an awkward, single-handed tying motion at his clavicle. "It'll keep you covered."

The part of her from before she was cursed urges her to take the talisman. The part of her from after, the part that matters because it's the part that's helped her survive, screams at her to push it away. Gifts, gestures of goodwill, random acts of kindness—she can't accept anything that risks forming even the thinnest spider's silk of connection between her and someone else. The stronger the connection, the more it hurts when eventually, inevitably, her curse rips it out at the roots.

"Damnit, Leathan." Renni's voice mirrors her desperation. "Let me do you one fucking favor."

A favor.

Favors are a gray area. Favors she can work with, if she returns them quickly enough, makes sure there's no time for sentimentality to fester.

She snatches the kerchief out of Renni's hand. "I owe you."

He barks a nasally laugh. "Don't worry about it."

"I'm not worried." Chin ducked, she knots the ends together behind her neck. The magic shapes the fabric, enveloping the pendant into its many folds. Her fingers itch to pick at the weave of the spell, to reverse engineer it.

She's still fussing with the kerchief when the giant prop sun sinks into the stage. Renni's cue. He hesitates on the balls of his feet. "You need me to—"

"You've done more than enough." She drops her hands, summons a confident smile to push him away. "Go."

He holds her gaze for a moment longer as if steeling them both, then disappears, all dazzle and easy grace, into the waiting spotlight. The roar of applause that greets him rattles the walls. Leathan hardly hears it over the frantic thrashing of her heart.

When her cue comes, a soft birdsong trilling of flute, she gives Renni's kerchief one last, surreptitious adjustment, and cartwheels to her mark.

Her pendant slides. Her gut lurches with it, but the charm in the fabric pulses featherlight magic and holds everything in place.

Renni spins in front of her. Glances at his handiwork, then shoots her a crooked tooth grin that makes him look about sixteen, even though he's at least thirty going on a hundred. Dizzy with relief, Leathan doesn't stop herself grinning back before shimmying up the high wires for the opening act.

Two

The big top is hazy with the audience's building energy. Pink anticipation, crimson excitement, amethyst yearning— a rainbow of emotion coils up from the mortals in clouds so thick, some of them might be able to perceive it. Unless they know anything of magic, though, Leathan suspects they'll attribute the nebulous hues to lighting effects.

Most of the energy flows to Renni, surrounding him in an iridescent halo. Rather than absorb it all himself, he deftly redirects it, both conducting the audience's suspended disbelief through the show—tailored around a local legend of doomed lovers—and ensuring every performer gets what they need to make quota. When she was first recruited, Leathan wasted many a breath trying to convince him she could manage fine on her own; now, she lets him think he's done his star-sworn duty by surreptitiously passing on whatever he sends her way to others who need it more.

As she twirls on the peripheral high wires, snatching up stray curls of yellow curiosity and lavender delight, her senses snag on an unsettling, familiar presence. She seizes the excuse to look away from the scene of the lovers' meet-cute on the giant teeterboard below, combing the two thousand faces in the darkened stands.

It takes her a single second to spot the Phenomenae spy.

Leathan doesn't know how she always finds them so quickly. The foreign signature of their ringmaster's magic is too weak and diffuse to pinpoint, a tiny itch on her senses that could easily be her imagination. Yet her gaze snaps to them like a magnet.

It must be the mask. Some fashionable mortals in the stands don thin plastic painted in stale acrylic, bought from an overpriced souvenir shop in town or perhaps one of the Extravaganza's own stalls. The spy's is nothing like that. From up in the wires, it's hard to make out any details other than sharp ears and an angled snout; but it must be spell-wrought, because she kens the artistry of its crafting.

Like she kens the intensity of the spy's eyes behind it, shadowing her every move.

She shouldn't blossom under the spotlight of their attention like she does. Shouldn't turn that extra turn for them, bend that extra centimeter, leap that much higher. Taunting an enemy, even an enemy as small as Phenomenae, even with the ceasefire holding steady for fifteen years, is asking for trouble. But weak ringmasters use spies to sniff out vulnerabilities to exploit, and Leathan refuses to show them anything but strength.

It's been like this every night since the Extravaganza arrived two months ago. A silent, focused struggle: the spy watching her like she's the only one on stage, her performing for them like they're the only one in the audience. The threat of their presence might distract someone else into fumbling a mark or missing quota, but Leathan always draws in enough to meet hers. In fact, this run has been her most lucrative yet.

Report *that* back to your ringmaster, spy.

Locked in the dance of their wordless war, Leathan doesn't register the rest of the show until the lovers are banished to stars on opposite ends of the universe, doomed to pine for one another from afar for the rest of eternity. The audience bursts into a standing ovation. The masked spy rises, too, the black holes of their eyes locked on Leathan through the prism of energy undulating through the big top.

Color crashes against Leathan in tidal waves as the troupers take their final bows. She absorbs as much as she can, a child trying to catch the ocean in a pail, blazing past her quota until the curtains swoop shut.

The energy in her compact thrums through her body, making her feel buoyant, like if she's not careful to stick the soles of her feet to the wooden slats of the floor, she's liable to float away. Backstage is a maelstrom of fireworks as the troupers' flamboyant costumes sparkle back into plain street clothes. The performers hug and high five, kiss, shout plans to meet up at the wrap party in the canteen, ramble about how they'll miss this city or how they can't wait for the next one.

Leathan finds her empty corner again, glad it's over, glad that this is their last night in town and the last night they have to perform the doomed lovers set and the last night she has to watch for the Phenomenae spy.

Yet an ache emanates from the part of her from before. Almost as if she'll miss them.

She ignores it.

Bravo, bravo. The troupers quiet when Yokuiv addresses them, though they don't need silence to hear him in their minds. Leathan gets a vision of him clapping long, lithe hands, a paternal smile curving his thin lips. The warmth of his satisfaction bathes her like gentle spring sunshine, and she can't help the contentment unfurling in her chest in response. *A splendid end to a record-breaking run.*

They go still, also unnecessary, as their ringmaster siphons from their compacts the energy they absorbed, and compensates them with an equivalent amount of his magic. For a moment the world is nothing but color and shimmering light, leaving Leathan breathless from the sheer wonder and weight of emotion.

The exchange complete, backstage roars to a frenzy now Yokuiv has fed and they've been paid for providing the meal. As soon as Leathan detaches her compact from her belly, her costume evanesces, and she's back in her buttoned blouse and pleated skirt. She peeks into her compact at the thimble-sized well of sparkling lihilim power within. Her minor part means her earnings are never much, even on lucrative nights like tonight—but magic is magic. She hopes it won't be another decade until she's saved enough to attempt breaking her curse again.

Assuming she doesn't strike out before then.

She tears Renni's kerchief from her neck, expecting to find him and his crooked tooth grin smack dab in the middle of the pandemonium, waiting for all the other troupers to leave before changing out of his costume; but she spots him on the peripheries, aurora borealis swirls and shimmer powder replaced with loose striped trousers and V-neck, flowing locs now a short-cropped, curly fade.

She catches him halfway through slipping out the back door. He startles at her touch, a brief flash of something crossing his face before it settles into his usual grin. "Hey— you were incredible out there, as always."

"Thanks for letting me borrow this." She thrusts the kerchief at him. He lifts one thick eyebrow and, infuriatingly, does not take it.

"Keep it." He sidles out the door, leaving her with the kerchief dangling from her outstretched fist, and a seed of connection rooting into her heart.

THREE

It took Leathan years until she learned to navigate the labyrinthine Extravaganza without getting lost. Yokuiv designed it to ensure circus-goers would meander the myriad stalls and tents, get sidetracked by sideshows, or double back for a snack. At the center towers the big top, a deceptive beacon seemingly just around the next corner—but never is until right before the show begins. A clever way to entice every last morsel of energy from their mortal guests.

Now her feet are swift down the familiar route to the backyard, the jumble of structures where the troupers live. She needs to store her pendant, and then figure out how to get this connection to Renni out of her before it sprouts.

It's blissfully quiet with their guests gone and the fairground troupers closing down their stalls, though it won't last once the wrap party gets going. As Leathan turns towards the storage shed, she kens, lingering in the air like perfume, magic. Foreign magic, but one whose signature—golden hour sun, sweet honeysuckle, soft down—she recognizes. The thrill of it sends a chill down the nape of her neck.

Phenomenae.

The spy.

They're out there, somewhere in the shadowed sea of stalls. It takes all Leathan's willpower not to crane her neck to look for them in the darkness. An ambush? Doubtful. Phenomenae magic is too weak to damage the Extravaganza, and even if that weren't the case, she can't believe the spy is reckless enough to try anything in the middle of enemy territory.

So why in the hells are they doing the magical equivalent of peeking around a corner and waving her over?

She should call for Yokuiv's construct guards. Raise the alarm an enemy is here, lingering within Extravaganza bounds after the outfit shut its gates for the night.

But curiosity nags at her, incessant. Against her better judgment, she follows the trail of magic through the labyrinth until it culminates at a shuttered candied fruits stall. The air is still sweet with molten sugar, sharp with the tang of ripe apples.

Cool fingers brush her elbow like a question.

She whirls and sees the spy up close for the first time.

They're a fox—their mask, that is, vermilion lacquer inlaid with twinkling jewels and seashell to give the illusion of fur, long snout revealing tiny canines painted with sharp precision. It is spell-wrought like Leathan thought; Phenomenae magic wafts off it like curls of incense. Leathan should begin the weave for—something—but she only stares and stares and stares, unblinking, silent and immobile.

The spy tilts their head, the sleek coils of their dark curls bouncing off their shoulders. The muzzle of their mask seems to curve into a smile. Leathan doesn't know if it bodes well or ill that they seem happy.

"Should one of us say something?" Their low voice is honey and velvet.

"Something." Hers is rusted nails.

Their barked laugh makes something with broken, jagged edges stir in Leathan's chest. She flinches. This was a bad idea, but turning tail now, in her own territory, will only make her look weak.

"My name's Zuna." They introduce themself so casually, like the two of them are benign strangers chatting in some queue. Like their ringmasters wouldn't have them at one another's throats if the ceasefire collapsed that very instant.

"Doubtless you already know mine."

"I do, but it's not as weird if you tell me."

She doesn't give them the satisfaction. "What the hells are you doing here?"

"I wanted to see you."

Whatever she was expecting, it wasn't that—and maybe that's why the spy said it. To throw her off balance. She steadies herself the same way she would on stage if she botched a move. Never let the audience catch you stumbling, and if they do, make sure they think it's all part of the performance. "You've seen me every night for two months."

"The show doesn't count." They step closer, the diaphanous jewel-tones of their clothing fluttering in the breeze. Leathan doesn't know if it's cowardice or courage keeping her feet rooted to the ground, but she doesn't move. She can make out every tiny painted detail of their mask. Her fingers itch to take it in hand, to examine each intricate twist of the magic woven into it, to understand how it was shaped and what it was shaped to do. She resists the urge. "I wanted to talk to you."

"I can't say the same."

"Liar," the spy purrs. "You didn't answer my call to glower and glare."

Glowering and glaring to prove that yes, that's *exactly* why she answered—never mind she has no idea of the real reason, but she's not going to pause to ponder—Leathan says, "Leave."

The spy's mask warps into a playful pout. "You'd deprive us of the pleasure of one another's company so soon?"

"Not soon enough."

"Ever the performer." Zuna lets out a sigh of mirth like wind through naked winter trees. It makes Leathan shiver, despite the muggy warmth of the night. "Arsenal of quips and comebacks at the ready so you never have to risk saying anything to reveal who you really are."

"That's rich coming from someone hiding behind a magic fox mask."

"I may be the one in the mask," they say, playfulness suddenly subdued, "but you're the one hiding."

Leathan's patience snaps. She grabs for her compact, ceasefire be damned, but the spy sinks into the shadows before she can finish weaving the hex. Though Leathan's looking right at them, her eyes go wobbly, and she loses sight of where they are. For once, she can't find them.

"We make quite the pair, don't you think?" Their whisper comes from over her shoulder. She whirls, magic dancing at the tips of her fingers—but they're gone, the signature of their ringmaster's magic dissipating into the dark with them.

"We don't make anything at all," she mutters, though the spy's no longer there to hear, or to call her a liar again.

With a frustrated growl, Leathan plucks the knots of the half-finished hex apart, spooling the unused magic back into her compact as she stomps through the backyard.

She wants nothing more than to get her pendant off from around her neck, but a fat mortal woman, her dark brown hair in a short bob, loiters in front of the storage shed, shooting nervous glances to the hulking humanoid construct guarding the entrance as she rummages through her purse. Leathan sucks in a long, labored breath. The Extravaganza's gates closed for the night ten minutes ago, though it feels like the detour with Zuna lasted hours. The mortal shouldn't be anywhere in the circus, let alone here.

She's not getting into any trouble, at least; if she were a threat, the construct would've dealt with her. It stands stoic and silent, unable to move unless there's immediate danger to the circus or Yokuiv issues it a command. An annoyed furrow carves deep lines in its white marble brow, mirroring Leathan's own mood.

"Oi," she snaps, short-tempered from dealing with one interloper that evening already. The mortal startles, clutching her scuffed purse to her chest as her brown cheeks pale and light green explodes around her. Leathan must've seriously spooked her. She ignores her guilt and the mortal's babbled excuses about being lost, jerking a thumb over her shoulder. "Exit's back there."

The mortal scampers away. Leathan gives a commiserative shake of her head to the construct as she waves her compact at it and heads inside the shed to store her pendant at long last. It says nothing, of course, all twelve of its pupil-less opal eyes staring after the woman, and the terror trailing in her wake.

FOUR

The thin siding of Leathan's tin can of a trailer does nothing to dull the roar of two hundred troupers reveling through the backyard. Ignoring the trio of trapeze artists making out beneath her front window, Leathan rummages through the hundred square feet she's lived in for the past ten years. She hasn't purged non-essentials this week yet; there's got to be something in here she can give Renni in exchange for the kerchief.

Her eyes flick again to the blue and brass fabric spilling out of her skirt pocket. She'd been too distracted to realize how much magic he'd used in the talisman's crafting, to even consider he'd make the charm last longer than the duration of the show—but there's enough for it to last months, maybe more. She should've tried harder to make him take it back.

Old aches stir beneath Leathan's ribs, as if she needs reminding what happens when she's not vigilant about preventing connections from taking root. What happens when her curse triggers and tears those connections out like so many weeds, taking chunks of her with them.

The memories of each time it happened are scabs she picks at when she's feeling especially self-destructive. The way one girl shrieked like a banshee when, as they watched an old animated film curled up on her living room floor, Leathan's bones broke and caved in on themselves. The string of expletives from a guy Leathan never heard utter a single dirty syllable, as they perused an outdoor market and in his hand her fingers withered to twigs. One person simply sat in stunned confusion, glasses slipping down the bridge of their nose, the dice they were about to roll clattering from their slack palm to the game board, as rusty red ichor bled from Leathan's eyes and nose.

And the last time—

The last time, she'd have died, if Yokuiv hadn't found her in a pool of blood and sap in some abandoned hovel at the ends of the earth, and offered her a contract then and there.

One of the trapeze artists lets out a moan of pleasure. Rubbing a fist against her sternum, Leathan regards the fruits of her scavenging: an old graphic novel with its cover taped together; capsule machine keychains; a palm-sized notepad missing its first few pages; a half-empty tube of her favorite apple-scented lotion.

After a minute chewing her lip, Leathan grabs the keychains. A twin set of glittering pastel rainbow cats with three eyes, they're the most valuable thing she has to offer in return for the kerchief. They were the secret prize, only one draw for every ten thousand attempts, if she read the accompanying strip of paper correctly. As an added bonus, they have the lowest risk of divulging anything too personal about herself, considering she got them on a whim while waiting to see that scam artist of a mystic.

But the keychains alone aren't enough. She reaches for her compact, begins to weave a charm into them. It's not a spell she's ever attempted, as far as she recalls. Weaving is the only time she allows the part of her from before to take a modicum of control, to move her fingers and shape the magic in ways she doesn't know how she knows.

It's pointless trying to remember things her curse made her forget. What she wants isn't her past, but her future. One where she can let an entire forest of connections grow wild in her heart without fear of consequence or pain.

The talisman complete, Leathan eases past the trapeze trio, who are too twisted up in pulled hair and biting lips to notice her. Long before she gets to Renni's trailer, she catches the bassline of a rock song thumping out of his window. Unlike her, he leaves his open to encourage the others to stop by and gossip over a cup of some tea or another. His burly silhouette sashays beyond the gauzy curtains as he styles his short-cropped curls and sings along with melodramatic gusto.

She snorts. He can't carry a tune to save his life, though that's never stopped him wasting vinyl to record his own demos. Which is why she charmed the keychains with perfect pitch.

"To what do I owe this rare pleasure?" Renni leans out the window, grinning his crooked tooth grin, pinching a cup of steaming golden tea at the rim between two fingers. The velvety scent of jasmine wafts over her; it smells divine, but she declines a cup when he offers.

It's a struggle not to smile back, but she's had years of practice. Focusing on the intricate tattoo of tentacles swirling in a wave that crashes from his left bicep to the thin, smooth scars beneath his pecs, she drops the kitty keychains onto the sill. "These are for you."

"Leathan ..." Renni cups the keychains in his free hand with gentle reverence, too many emotions flitting across his features to name. A gleam in his eyes looks suspiciously like tears. "You've never given me a gift before."

She shrugs like it's no big deal, because it isn't; just a balancing of the scales. Already she can feel the tendrils binding him to her heart loosening. "Don't get used to it."

"Brat. Catch you at the wrap party?" Renni calls as she heads for the showers. "You promised you'd go this time."

"I promised I'd think about it."

"You better be there. You can only keep up this aloof loner thing for so long."

She pats the air in a placating *yeah, yeah,* and takes the back way to the showers to scrub this shit day off her.

After, auburn hair in damp scraggles and white skin smelling of apples, she grabs a quick dinner from the canteen while the rest of the Extravaganza are too preoccupied with their fun to notice her slip in and out. When Renni asks her tomorrow as they prep for relocation, she can tell him she went to the party without lying.

Belly sated if not quite full, she hurries back to the safety of her trailer. As she rounds the corner, the pulsating party lights behind her give her a glimpse of a ruddied, bearded face before the big illusionist it belongs to slams straight into her. She stumbles; the illusionist grabs her by the elbow before she falls on her ass.

"Watch it," he snaps before striding off into the dark, away from her and the party. Leathan glares after him, holding her shoulder. Her bruised muscles throb in the brief moment it takes her contractual protections to heal them. The fuck is his problem?

A strangled shout splits the air.

Leathan's running towards it before she realizes her legs are moving. Her thoughts flash to Zuna, to their grinning fox's mask and the shadows enveloping them in a lover's embrace. She's felt no trace of their magic in hours, assumed they'd gone back to their outfit—was she wrong? Had they stayed? Have they hurt someone?

Has someone hurt them?

It isn't the spy she finds, but a petite contortionist on her hands and knees in the small plot of grass in front of Renni's trailer, flinging a distress weave towards their ringmaster's office. Leathan sidesteps the beetle-shaped beacon as it skitters past and rushes to help the contortionist up.

Tears sleeting down her gaunt face, the contortionist clutches at Leathan with one hand and signs frantically with the other. The acid in Leathan's stomach curdles; she can't be understanding correctly—turns to Renni's trailer to be sure—and wishes she didn't.

The door swings open on creaking hinges. In the threshold a lamp lies on its side, shade knocked askew, flickering bulb casting low, sharp angles over a spreading pool of blood.

FIVE

The world bucks and sways like a ship on a gale. Leathan's balance abandons her; she swoons over the arm of a chair, dark fireworks exploding at the edges of her vision. The contortionist is gone; Renni's trailer is gone.

Renni is gone.

Dead.

No. He can't be. None of them can die. They can be hurt, sure, but as long as they're contracted to the Extravaganza, they can't die.

Not easily.

All that blood—

Renni's not even in his trailer. He's at the party. Leathan saw him holding court when she grabbed dinner at the canteen.

Didn't she?

She wracks her brain, but the last clear memories she has of him are the kitty keychains cradled in his palm, the playful tenor of his voice calling her a brat as she walked away.

The scent of petrichor fills her nose. As it ebbs, her surroundings come to her piecemeal: a small mahogany writing desk sandwiched by two plush chairs, a collection of strange liquor on the windowsill, a beat-up cabinet in the far corner beside a spiraling stairway.

Her ringmaster kneels in front of her.

Leathan stares in open fascination, doesn't try not to. Lihilim are every human desire made flesh—and what mere human has the strength of will to look away from everything they've ever wanted?

She's seen his true lihilim form once before, the day he recruited her into his service. He'd appeared like a beacon in the storm then, and in him she'd seen sanctuary and safety, all the soft things she thought her curse had stolen from her forever; but now the ethereal shape of him looks more like a warning. He purses his lips as he surveys her with summer sun intensity. His skin, pale as pearls, emits a smoldering glow, blue eyes impossibly large and round, hands long and lithe and capped in talon-like nails, feathered wings folded still and sanguine behind broad shoulders.

"Drink this." A crystal tumbler full of a fizzing golden liquid appears beneath her face. Yokuiv folds her limp fingers around the glass, tips it towards her lips. Her tongue tingles with sharp pops of ginger laced with bittersweet notes of his magic. "You've had quite the shock."

Her ringmaster holds her like a nursing babe until she downs the last drop. Stiffly, she straightens, feeling as if she's been pulled apart and pieced back together. Yokuiv had been enchanting her, she realizes. Sifting out her memories of the evening. Hours have passed since she found the contortionist in front of Renni's trailer. She feels them hit her all at once, exhaustion pulling at the corners of her eyes, cramping her gut, fevering her skin. She wants to go to sleep, to wake up and have this all be a horrible nightmare.

"Renni," she mewls, part question, part plea.

"I'm sorry." Yokuiv inclines his head, and with that simple gesture her world threatens to break all over again. "I swear I will find his killer, but I will need your help."

Fighting back nausea, struggling to make sense of this new reality where she is and Renni is not, Leathan stammers, "Why?"

"You're the only one I trust not to let personal biases interfere." Yokuiv plucks a second tumbler out of the air and fills it with a generous splash of dark amber liquid from a bottle on the sill. A melange of mortal energies, aged or fermented or processed somehow by lihilim techniques into a soothing, inebriating substance. "Friendly enough as you are, you aren't actually friends with anyone else in my outfit."

Which is the exact balance she's worked so hard to maintain since she joined, but he puts such a fine point on it that it pierces through her. She grinds her teeth against the sting before realizing he didn't bring it up to be cruel. "You think an Extravaganza trouper murdered him."

"No mortal could have done this."

Despite her ringmaster's certainty, she can't think of a single trouper who'd wish Renni harm. Unlike Leathan, he is—was—friends with everyone in the outfit. Everyone besides her.

"What about—" She catches herself before she calls Zuna by name, unsure if her meeting with them was one of the memories Yokuiv pulled from her, and not wanting to explain if it wasn't. She doesn't think he'd be angry, but it's fraught territory she's not keen to tread. "The Phenomenae spy?"

Yokuiv's lips curve into a cold smile at the rim of his glass. "A buzzing fly from a weak, shambling corpse of an outfit. That they could have worked magic strong enough to kill one of mine—could have so much as *thought* about

working any magic in my domain without my knowledge—
is impossible."

Relief floods Leathan with his backhanded assertion of
the spy's innocence, followed by confusion. Why should
she be glad it's not them?

She focuses instead on something else that makes no
sense. She knows better than to assume her ringmaster
hasn't already enchanted the entire troupe as he did her.
"But you didn't find the memory of the—the act—in
anyone's mind."

Frustration warping his features, Yokuiv picks up a
slender, silver disc from his desk. An old-fashioned film
reel, redolent with magic. "Perhaps I'm somehow mistaken,
and the killer isn't among you; but I think it more likely
there are details, however small or insignificant, I can't see
from my perspective. Which is why I want yours."

"You want me to relive everyone's memories?" The idea
makes her queasier than the aftereffects of his enchantment.
She presses into the seat, as far away from the film reel as
she can get.

"Only the most relevant. I am, of course, offering fair
compensation." With a flick of his hand, one of the drawers
in the corner cabinet slides open. Out floats a scroll of
yellowed parchment. A contract—*her* contract. Three
scarlet wax insignia seal it shut. Two are slashed through. Is

it her imagination, or is a spider's silk crack beginning at the rippled edges of the third? "Help me find the killer, and I can make these whole."

Her throat goes dry. She never knew strikes could be reversed, but there's a lot she doesn't know about the circuses or ringmasters or lihilim, even after ten years. She won't approach anyone to ask. All she's learned she's picked up through observation and eavesdropping, fitted together into an incomplete picture with gaping holes.

One thing she does know is curses don't take kindly to being captured and diminished, and the longer they stew in their wrath, the more vengeful they become. When a trouper completes the hundred-year term of their contract, ringmasters extract their curse so it's no more and no less powerful than before its imprisonment. But if they strike out, the pendant shatters. The difference between venting pressure from a sealed container, and it exploding all at once.

It happened to Renni's predecessor, Orrus. Yokuiv was able to contain the damage, though not before the rogue curse tore Orrus limb from limb.

It's what would've happened to Leathan, if she hadn't accepted the kerchief from Renni.

The blue and brass fabric is in her hands before she realizes she's drawn it out of her pocket. Perhaps she's been clutching it all night and hasn't noticed. Are her fingers numb from folding and unfolding the magicked fabric between them for hours on end, or from what Yokuiv is asking her to do?

Because what Yokuiv is asking her to do risks everything she's been avoiding since she joined. The clean slate he's offering won't matter if she can't break her curse before finishing her contract; her curse may not tear her limb from limb, but it will tear out every connection she lets sprout between her and any of the others—and seeing things through their eyes, attempting to *understand* them, is fertile ground for connection to blossom.

Yet as she fusses with the kerchief, she's horrified to feel one connection worming through her: fondness for Renni, rooted even deeper than before, and she knows there's only one thing she can do to prune it out for good.

Find his killer. Find who did this, and make them pay.

"No promises." She knots the kerchief around her left wrist. "But I'll try."

Yokuiv smiles grimly. "Good. I'd hoped you wouldn't waste more time agreeing. We only have until dawn."

Her mouth falls open. "That's—"

"Not long from now, no. I suspect the killer chose our final evening of the run to strike on purpose, wagering I wouldn't be able to complete my investigation before we relocate."

"The Greater Circuit still expects us to leave on schedule?"

"What they do and don't expect runs counter to most logical thought." He drowns his disdain in another drink and motions for her to follow him out of his office. "I've petitioned them for an emergency extension, but rest little hope upon it. Troupe overlap apparently risks reigniting the war, and they prioritize preserving their precious ceasefire above all else. Even bringing a murderer to justice."

SIX

Among the looming shapes of the Extravaganza backyard, so distorted in the starless dark, Leathan's exhausted mind brings her back to the day she joined. Yokuiv led her to the trailers then, too, walking so slow that bright October afternoon she nearly stepped on the heels of his polished leather shoes a dozen times in her impatience.

Now she has to jog to keep up.

"Relax," then-Yokuiv soothed when she flinched at a stray breeze teasing the scrabbles of her hair. He lifted the corner of a silk square to show her, freshly forged and gleaming in the palm of his hand, her pendant. The tumbleweed twigs he'd clipped from her not an hour past cycloned inside, shorn ends scratching trails of red sap against the gold filigreed glass. "Your curse cannot harm you as long as you belong to my Extravaganza. Nothing can."

Then how is it Renni's dead?

Half a dozen constructs stand in a barricade around Renni's trailer, their eyes roaming the darkened backyard. Out of thin air, an antique tripod projector unfurls with a snap of metal hinges and a shockwave of dust. Leathan smothers a pair of sneezes in her elbow as Yokuiv positions the device before taking the ensorcelled film out of its reel and feeding it into the mechanism. He flips a switch on the top, and with a clatter, the device casts a dome of grainy, sepia-toned light over the trailer.

Images shift and settle like silt sinking to the bottom of a pond. Yokuiv swipes two fingers in a quick circle, as if winding a dial, and the projection flickers. Dozens of troupers zip to and from Renni's open window at dizzying speed. It's so fast Leathan can't pick them all out in individual detail, but she glimpses a gaggle of knife throwers, the amorous trapeze trio, some jugglers, a couple of clowns.

"Such a popular boy," her ringmaster muses. "Does half my Extravaganza always stop by his trailer after a show?"

Leathan shakes her head as the ghostly version of herself drops the kitty keychains on the sill. "Usually he stays backstage until everyone else leaves, but tonight he left early to get ready for the wrap party."

"I see." Her ringmaster curls his fingers like a flower furling its petals. Time slows to normal speed. Renni's window is closed now, but the light's still on inside, the music so loud the bassline pounds through Leathan's chest. Out from the trailer opposite Renni's strides the bearded illusionist Leathan ran into earlier. Instinctively she sidesteps out of the way as the big man stomps up to bang, rapid-fire, on Renni's door.

"Turn it down, asshole," the illusionist bellows over a guitar swell. He pounds his thick fist on the door again when there's no reply. Anticipatory bile claws up Leathan's throat. Is Renni dead already?

"In a second," the star calls at last. Leathan releases a trembling breath, even though she knows there's no reason to be relieved. "You know I've always loved this song, Berhede."

The illusionist grinds his teeth on the first blustered syllable of a retort. Nostrils flaring so wide Leathan half expects smoke to curl out of them, he thrusts both middle fingers at the curtained window and sulks off into the backyard. She touches her shoulder, feeling the phantom ache of where he'd barreled into her. "Something tells me that was about more than just music."

Her ringmaster hums pensively. The song stops. Leathan's ears ring in the silence as the petite contortionist from earlier flits to where Berhede had been standing. Her hands flick in front of her stomach in lightning-fast signs. Leathan catches snippets: "I know you," something, something, "work it out," something, something.

Adjusting her ruched black dress, the contortionist raps her knuckles against the door. Waits a few seconds, tries again. When there's still no answer, she tries the handle. It's unlocked.

Leathan twitches as if to stop the contortionist slipping inside, but there's nothing she can do to change what's going to happen. What's already happened.

The light inside the trailer strobes. There's a crash. The door slams open; the contortionist bursts out with a scream, misses the first step and slams to the ground. Her ruby red compact bounces out of her grip. She scrambles after it on hands and knees, halfway through weaving a distress signal when the projection flickers and vanishes.

Yokuiv strides to the trailer door.

"Leathan," he prompts, when she makes no move to follow.

"Can't you—" She swallows. She doesn't want to see Renni's body, but there's more making her hesitate. She's never been inside anyone else's trailer before. Never let anyone inside hers. "Describe it to me?"

"You're here to tell me what you see, not the other way around. Come, or this entire exercise is moot."

Leathan reminds herself she agreed to this. Focuses on the image of her contract, of all three of its seals whole. Spins Renni's kerchief around her wrist until she gives herself friction burns, which her contractual protections heal so all she's left with is an uncomfortable warmth on her skin.

She goes inside.

Seven

Renni's trailer is no bigger than Leathan's. She always thought it'd be more spacious, considering he's their star—was their star—but it's the same size, the same layout. As far as she can tell, underneath all the mess, and all the blood.

More clothes than she's owned her entire life avalanche out of the closet's sliding door to the foot of his vanity, atop which an ancient metal teapot and chipped ceramic cup float in a cluttered sea of cosmetics. His battered old record player perches beneath the window on low shelves crammed with teas of all sorts, their scents mingling with the peppermint and shea of his hair gel. Faded Extravaganza magic frosts everything with a transparent, glittery sheen.

There's so much *stuff* she almost misses, nestled like a compass needle in the middle of the carpet between piles of dirty laundry and towers of tattered vinyl albums, the severed arm.

Transfixed in horror, she stares at the rounded stump of exposed shoulder bone, the shorn-off tattoo on the bicep. She always wondered why Renni chose that wave and tentacle design. The ink is neon bright against ashy, waxen skin.

The longer she looks, the less real it seems. *That could be anyone's arm,* Leathan wants to say. Instead, she drags her gaze away and chokes out, "Where's the rest of him?"

Yokuiv lets out a chortle, low and mirthless. "It's remarkable anything of him is left at all. The sheer amount of raw power required to circumvent a trouper's contractual protections should eradicate every trace of them from reality. This is sloppy work."

"It's not." Embarrassment sears Leathan's face when her ringmaster regards her with raised eyebrows. "I mean, the whole career's worth of magic sprayed over the place aside, it's pretty contained. Shouldn't there be signs of struggle, or counterspells? Defensive measures?"

"One would imagine." Soft surprise tinges her ringmaster's agreement. He drags one hand along his narrow jaw and mulls over the trailer. "Yet there are none. How strange. Renni was one of my best soldiers; I'd assumed he fought back."

Leathan stares at Renni's empty, curled fingers, then casts around the trailer, circling around it like the single hand of a slow clock. So much stuff, but one thing is missing. "Maybe he couldn't. His compact's gone. They must've taken it."

"Perhaps." Yokuiv picks up Renni's arm, hefting it like he's trying to approximate its weight before replacing it and pressing his own palm into the carpet. Blood and weak sparks of magic well up around his hand. His eyes sharpen. "There is something here."

He rubs his stained fingers together, then drags the tip of his pinky across his lips. Leathan cries out in disgust, though Yokuiv doesn't notice. His beautiful features warp in distaste, and he lets out a sharp exhalation before proffering his bloodstained hand to her.

When she balks, he gives her a sardonic half-smile. "Imbibing it as I have would tell you little. I'm curious what human perception might reveal."

Nothing more than what he kens of his own power, surely—but as long as she doesn't have to put Renni's blood in her mouth, she doesn't see the harm in examining the spell. Gingerly, Leathan reaches out her senses to the traces of magic mingled with the blood. The spell isn't one she's familiar with, not that she expects to identify it; but a subtle bitterness accompanying it sparks vague recognition. A halting staleness in the way it slips and slides along her awareness, warm and acrid. "It's ... evasive. Like grasping at clouds."

"Smog, more appropriately." Yokuiv gives one sharp flick of his hand. Droplets of blood and magic skid off his pale skin like water off a slick leaf. "Corrupted as it is."

Leathan's not convinced the alterations tip over into the realm of corruption, but she chews her bottom lip to stop herself arguing semantics. The real concern is an Extravaganza trouper is capable of not just manipulating threads of lihilim power, but changing those threads' very properties—albeit akin to something as superficial as the color, but she'd have dismissed it as impossible before kenning it herself. "If you forget what they used it for, it's kind of impressive they managed to hold it long enough to make the weave in the first place ..."

Curiosity tempts her into reaching for the magic a second time. She identifies no structure, no pattern, no knots or folds. There are—ripples? Too smooth and continuous to be a weave at all. More like—a distillation. Like it's been dissolved in liquid. Again that bitterness laps at her senses.

"Tea." She whirls to the cup on Renni's vanity, snatching it up. There's a scattering of dark leaves at the bottom. She brings it to her nose for a tentative sniff. The strong fragrance of roasted leaves and herbs is nothing like the gentle jasmine he'd been drinking when she'd stopped by his trailer earlier. Nothing like any blend he favors, in fact. It's so strong she almost misses the traces of the evasive magic she kenned in Renni's blood. She jerks back, rubs her nose on her sleeve. "They poisoned his tea."

EIGHT

A brown paper pouch lays on its side beside the teapot, its label torn off. The instant Leathan cracks the keep-fresh seal, she knows it's the blend in the cup. It smells even stronger dried, strong enough she can taste it on the back of her tongue, that it's all she smells even once she's resealed the pouch. Strong enough to cloak the telltale signature of malicious magic until it's too late.

There's no magic in the pouch, so the killer didn't poison the leaves, but the brew. Which means someone was inside his trailer—someone Renni let inside. The trailer's far too cramped to sneak around in unnoticed, and there's no need to sneak anyway, since Renni was always happy to have people in for a drink and a chat.

Whoever it was must've brought it with them, a weapon disguised as an end-of-run gift—brewed it for him themself, even, slipped the poison into his cup when Renni wasn't looking. But Yokuiv had showed her no memories of anyone going into his trailer except the contortionist, and that was after he'd been killed.

Tea, cup, and questions in hand, Leathan turns to her ringmaster—but he's gone. She takes the excuse to hurry out of the trailer herself.

Warmth like sun on a cold morning tingles across her skin; the scent of powdered granite melts on her tongue; tiny, delicate flower petals dance across her vision. Leathan's so relieved to be out of Renni's trailer, it takes her a few seconds to ken the sensations as the signature of unfamiliar lihilim magic.

The stranger it belongs to has their hands tucked into trailing sleeves over their big belly as they watch Yokuiv read a letter bearing the Greater Circuit's crest. The same gently spinning knot of circles hovers at the center of their forehead, speckling their face with prismatic, ever-shifting freckles. Their obsidian skin and wings emanate a vibrant violet glow in the pastel light filtering across the eastern skies, raven-down hair a fluffy, jewel-studded halo about their plump features.

This is the second time in a day Leathan's been dazzled by unadulterated lihilim beauty—the first time ever she's seen a lihilim who isn't her ringmaster. When they notice her stunned attention, their black eyes crinkle behind huge, golden-framed spectacles. The tender smile is such a fleeting break in their otherwise beatific expression, she's half-convinced she imagined it.

With a dissatisfied growl, Yokuiv crumples the paper in one fist. "'Fuck you, get out of the territory'—is that how I'm to understand this drivel?"

"Fuck you, get out of the territory *please*," amends the Circuit representative.

The paper bursts into flame, scorched by an intensity of raw power Yokuiv doesn't bother weaving into a spell. There's nothing to show the letter ever existed, no smudge of ash or whiff of smoke.

Oh. *That's* why he called Renni's killer sloppy.

Unfazed, the representative nudges their spectacles up their wide nose. "You are welcome to lodge objections with the Circuit after you've relocated."

"Which, as I explained in my original message, Igmun, assuming the Circuit bothered to read it, I am most happy to do," the Extravaganza ringmaster says, scathing and sarcastic, looming centimeters from the representative, "once I've concluded the investigation of my star's murder."

Igmun straightens the finger they'd used to adjust their spectacles, the tiny gesture demarcating a clear boundary between the two lihilim. "*Alleged* murder."

"I fail to understand how a severed arm, several liters of blood, and expenditure of a full compact's worth of my power could be construed as anything else."

"An accident developing a new spell, a curse breaking gone awry, gods forbid the poor man took matters into his own hands—any number of things might account for your star's untimely demise. Humans are so terribly fragile and finite." Igmun sighs, as if they wish that weren't the case. "Judging from your own account—your message was read, I assure you—nothing points to foul play except your word, and your word doesn't hold as much sway as it once did. They want evidence."

Something sharp and brittle flashes in Yokuiv's bright blue eyes. In the seething second before he can respond, Leathan forces herself forward. "Um."

Both lihilims' gazes snap to her, and even though she braced for this, she still quails like a hare caught between two hounds. Tightening her grip on the teacup and pouch, she holds them up. The world's flimsiest sword and shield. "If the Circuit wants evidence, this is it. Someone gave him this tea to cover up the taste of corrupted magic."

Triumph sparks in her ringmaster's features as Igmun's thick brow furrows. The Circuit crest hovering at their forehead wobbles on its axis as they examine the teacup. Their features warp in the same expression of distaste as

Yokuiv. "There is nothing to say he did not poison the tea himself."

"But then who disintegrated the rest of his body? Stole his compact?" Leathan's audacity comes easily with her ringmaster looking on in approval and Renni's kerchief tingling with protective magic around her wrist. "Even if he were the kind of person to do this to himself, which he isn't, poison doesn't account for that."

"It is as I implored the Circuit," Yokuiv says gravely. "There is more to this I need time to find."

Tapping their forearms inside their long sleeves, Igmun considers trouper and ringmaster for a long moment. At last their eyelashes flutter shut in grudging acquiescence. "You must secure Phenomenae's permission to remain."

"Permission." The Extravaganza ringmaster spits the word like a curse. "From that insignificant farce of an outfit? The wolf might as well ask permission to dwell in the woods from a rotting twig."

"Yet ask you must," Igmun says, diplomatic, apologetic, though Leathan senses the threat even before they unsheathe it, "or be found in violation of the ceasefire, stripped of rank and outfit, and—"

"Yes, yes, I am aware," Yokuiv snaps. He inhales through his aquiline nose, lets his long eyelashes flutter shut, rolls his neck in slow circles. "I will arrange for my absence."

"Splendid. I shall fetch Abidine and await you at the tables. Don't tally too long, or I shall be forced to assume you've reconsidered." With one final, benevolent smile, Igmun spins on their heel and vanishes.

Yokuiv utters something swift and breathless in the lihilim tongue. Beautiful and melodic as it sounds, Leathan can't imagine it means anything kind.

"You've done well, Leathan." He eases the teacup from her grip, holding it up to the light like that could help him see through its mysteries. She suppresses another flinch when he folds his fingers around hers and the waxed paper tea pouch crunches. "But this only brings us one step closer to the killer. While I am—politicking, you must speak to your colleagues. Find out where this tea came from, and what else they are hiding."

"How?" Panic and exhaustion threaten to consume her. First he asked her to relive their memories; now he wants her to *talk* to them? "I might as well be a complete stranger."

Her ringmaster gives her a cunning smile, tucks a loose scraggle of hair behind her ear, and strokes smooth knuckles down her cheek. Power trails in the wake of his touch, rich and warm, effervescing the exhaustion throbbing behind her eyes and gumming up her bones. She feels alert and nimble, as if she's gotten the best night's sleep she's ever had; yet she's far from relaxed. Every refreshed muscle in her body tenses, waiting for the trap she knows she's caught in to spring.

"I think you'll find them more than willing to share their secrets," says Yokuiv, satisfied, "now they will believe you to be one of their closest friends."

Decades of curating careful distance between her and the others, dismantled in a single instant. He might as well have destroyed her as thoroughly as the letter from the Circuit. She wants to scream. She wants to make him unravel the charm. All she can manage is a petulant frog-croak of, "How long?"

"Until the culprit is caught." Her ringmaster summons a lightweight cloak out of thin air, the navy cashmere embellished with embroidery and gems. "Be warned, the charm is mere illusion—powerful and persuasive, but illusion nonetheless. You must do your part to keep it from breaking. Perform the role. You are capable enough, or I wouldn't have assigned you to the big top."

Yokuiv's right; she *is* good at performing. She's done that her whole life—or as far back as her curse lets her remember, which amounts to the same thing. The charm will only make her audience more willing, more receptive, to her act.

"I should return shortly." As Yokuiv swirls the cloak over his wings, his collared shirt and fitted slacks snap themselves into freshly pressed creases, his blond hair slicks itself back into place, and his pale eyes reclaim their cheerful glint with no lingering embers of fury. She's not the only seasoned performer here. "Until then, I want business as usual. The show must go on."

Without Renni—without their star—Leathan doesn't see how it can.

NINE

With Yokuiv's charm humming in her veins even as his absence gnaws at the edge of her senses, Leathan hurries to her trailer to swap her day-old street clothes for training sweats. Hopefully she's swift enough to make it to the gym first, to have a few moments alone to steel herself before she has to pretend she's everyone's best friend.

It's barely dawn and already the humidity is so stifling she can't draw a full breath. Despite the pallid mist clinging to the circus like cotton candy, everything seems too crisp, too real. Her focus swirling from her impending transformation into social butterfly, to severed arms, to corrupted magic and the pouch of tea stuffed in her back pocket, habit takes her past Renni's trailer again before she can think to take a detour.

The constructs guarding it are curled up in the front yard in a heap, twitching beneath a shimmering net of

Extravaganza magic. Instinct makes Leathan dodge for cover against the side of the trailer. She flips open her compact and angles the mirror so she can peek around the corner without being spotted. A single construct is far from easy prey, let alone six of them, yet here they are, trussed up like marionettes tangled in their own strings. She can't fathom the amount of power that required, or the skill and speed to take the constructs out before they raise other alarms.

But she can venture a guess at who's responsible, and why. The same trouper who killed Renni, returned to the scene of the crime to clean up evidence they'd left behind. The tea?

Or something else Leathan missed?

So slow and silent she would've never noticed if she hadn't been looking, the trailer door cracks open.

Despite her suspicions, despite what she saw and found inside, she's half-convinced it's going to be Renni, hair and make-up perfect because it's always perfect, water bottle in one hand and golden compact in the other as he stretches a yawn to the lightening sky.

Out of the trailer slips a short, round figure, their face hidden in their hood, one arm bundled around something awkward and bulky. It isn't him. Of course it isn't him.

Leathan recoils when the figure glances furtively around. Satisfied the coast is clear, they dart away, keeping to the weedy grass to dampen their footsteps. Leathan follows, silent thanks to the decades she's had to practice moving without drawing attention to herself. She could call to them like the friend Yokuiv's charm will make them believe she is—but eventually they'll go into their own trailer and reveal their identity. Better if she can learn who they are without exchanging a single word.

The figure leaves the cluster of trailers without slowing, and Leathan's stomach lurches like she's misstepped on the high wire. They're beelining for the circus threshold. She doesn't have her pendant to follow them out, can't fetch it without losing sight of them.

Yokuiv's charm nudges her in the ribs, urging her out into the looming spotlight.

Nerves jittering the way they did before her first show in the big top, free hand clutching at the knot of Renni's kerchief, Leathan sucks in as deep a breath she can. "Morning."

The figure whips around. Leathan offers her best approximation of Renni's crooked tooth grin—the one that made it seem like running into you was the highlight of his existence—when a puff of startled orange energy jolts off the figure's tensed shoulders.

It's not an Extravaganza trouper under that hood, but a mortal.

A guffaw bubbles out of Leathan's mouth. She should be, if not scared, at least *concerned* a mortal wielding Extravaganza magic slipped into the circus undetected, disabled half a dozen constructs, and stole from Renni's trailer—but all Leathan feels is relief this means they aren't susceptible to Yokuiv's charm, and don't believe them to be friends.

The opposite, in fact, which is made apparent when they fling something small and dense with power at Leathan's face.

Her body moves before her brain. She weaves a defensive spell and bats the projectile away. It slams into a stack of crates to her left, bursting into sticky slime that trails down the side paneling in expanding streaks.

The mortal dashes towards the reality outside the Extravaganza. In their haste their hood falls back. The glimpse Leathan gets—short brown hair pulled into a short stub at the nape of the neck, anxious features lined with middle age—itches in her memory. She's seen this mortal before.

Last night, loitering outside the storage shed, claiming to be lost.

Leathan lassos magic around the mortal's ankle. She stumbles, crying out as she loses her grip on the bundle in her arms and it flies out of the quilted cloth it's wrapped in.

Brass light glints off the burnished turntable as Renni's record player cartwheels into the air. The mortal's energy follows it, a thick cocktail of terrified greens and nauseous bruise-purples.

Without thinking Leathan hurtles past the mortal's prone form and catches the player before it can smash upon the ground. It's still warm from the mortal's body heat, tingling all over with Extravaganza magic. As she adjusts her grip around the player, its needle falls onto the record still somehow firmly on deck, scratching out a handful of thin, reedy notes.

"I'm sorry I can't be honest," a soft tenor sings. Leathan goes as still as a construct to hear Renni's voice, so close and clear and perfectly in tune. He must've recorded this demo after she'd given him the keychains.

Before his killer struck.

The mortal wriggles free of the spell's bindings and pelts a fistful of beads at Leathan. They explode in a haze of smoke and percussive gut-punch of power that knocks her onto her ass. Leathan skids head over heels in the dirt, cushioning the player from harm with her body.

"In my dreams I tell you everything," Renni sings. Bravado reverberates up her arms.

As she scrambles upright, the mortal hurls yet another talisman imbued with Extravaganza power. It cracks open on her skull. Magic oozes out of it like raw egg, sharp and astringent, jolting Leathan to her core.

She flops to the ground like a fish in an electrified net, every muscle jerking and jumping. Her contractual protections buffer her against the pain, heals her scrapes and bruises from the fall; but it can't stop the hex immobilizing her.

Her compact rolls away into the grass. Her grip on the record player goes slack. The mortal snatches it from her useless fingers, moves the needle off the record. The demo stops.

"Rnnh," Leathan tries to call out, tries to inch-worm towards her compact; but the more she struggles, the more the hex digs into her, rendering her limp and impotent.

"I'm sorry," whispers the mortal. Oddly enough, Leathan believes she means it.

Not like it matters when she can do nothing but watch her flee past the threshold.

TEN

As the mortal woman's energy dissipates into the dawn, Leathan hears the crunch of feet against gravel. For one brief moment she hopes it's a construct pursuing the mortal past the threshold; then Yokuiv's charm reaches out like a vine winding towards the sun, and her insides wither.

She whimpers as the charm curls around the trouper kneeling beside her. The hex makes her vision swim, but she glimpses towering stripes of candy-bright fabric stretched across taught muscles, red hair looping like licorice twists around a tawny face painted whipped-cream white. Aqi, her panicking brain supplies. One of the trapeze artists making out by her trailer last night. As big as e is, e looks small without eir lovers wrapped in eir arms.

"Holy hells—Leathan—" It's been so long since she's heard her name spoken by anyone other than Yokuiv or Renni, it sounds like a foreign word. Aqi fumbles for the bubblegum pink compact embedded into the sash at eir thick waist, but Leathan grunts as loud as the hex will allow, jerking her chin in the direction of her own pearlescent clamshell nestled in the grass not an arm's length away. "It's okay, I know how to frog a hex off someone else. Me and Vetsla and Te'ide got each other out of plenty during the war."

She grunts and jerks her chin again, despite the retaliatory jolt from the hex. She's supposed to pretend to be eir friend, and a friend would accept eir help without argument, but she's too rattled—not by the hex, but Yokuiv's charm making Aqi call her by name, not to mention she somehow knows *eirs* despite having never spoken to em. Even if whatever connection her ringmaster's charm builds between them is artificial and hollow and impermanent, it's too much, too fast.

Relenting, Aqi flips open her compact and slides it into her hand. It takes Leathan a couple tries to crook her fingers at the right angle to craft a counterspell, and a few more to wheedle into the hex's weave. The knots are small but loose, thankfully, or she'd be spending the rest of the morning frogging it apart. As it is, her concentration frays around the numb stream of *friends, e believes we're friends* in her head, and the connection between them burning raw and red in her chest—but the hex shudders under her methodical unraveling until it relaxes around her throat.

Aqi's eyes narrow as e watches her struggle her shoulders free next. "Are you sure you don't want me to—"

"Why are you in costume?" The diverting question oozes out viscous as mud. Leathan gags and drags her teeth along her tongue to scrape away the magic's slimy aftertaste.

"I saw you lying there—after what happened to Renni, I thought …" Magic fizzing at their fingertips, the trapeze artist swivels around as if expecting the killer to attack at any moment. "Bad luck to go into battle without changing."

It feels like every other day Leathan learns about a new circus superstition: certain gestures to encourage extra energy before stepping out on stage, no looking backwards during a relocation, never making direct eye contact with mortal guests. "My attacker booked it past the threshold. Relax."

Aqi gives a non-committal huff, pausing eir vigil to rake chocolate brown eyes over the half-woven hex tangled around her. "Not with one of us going around pulling stunts like this the instant Yokuiv leaves the outfit."

"It wasn't one of us." With great effort, Leathan wrests one arm out of the hex's grip to pick up the spent talisman. Devoid of magic, it's nothing but a pinky-sized pouch of patterned purple silk. Stitches form hurried dashes along the joined edges except for the corner where they've split and frayed, a casualty of the imbued magic bursting out. Decent work; it'd be as good as the kerchief Renni made her, if it weren't so rushed. "Mortal hit me with this after I caught her stealing from Renni's trailer."

Something—guilt, recognition, anger?—flashes across Aqi's features. "Was it a woman with short brown hair? Round face, middle-aged?"

Leathan's surprised enough to stop slicing her way free. "How'd you know?"

"Call it an educated guess." The trapeze artist goes to stroke a beard that's no longer there—e shaved it off weeks ago, complaining of the valley heat—and instead scratches short fingernails along eir smooth jaw. "Since we started this run, Renni'd been dealing with an 'impassioned fan,' as he called her. Stalker, more like it. She'd get here too early, leave too late, follow him around the circus, bide her time so she could get him alone ..."

"That's—" Words like *horrible* and *terrible* don't seem fitting enough. "I had no idea."

"He never wanted to worry anyone, did he?" The sympathetic smile e offers grates against her already abused nerves. "I wouldn't have known either, if I hadn't caught her cornering him outside the big top last night. I *knew* I should've had a construct throw her out, but she scampered off as soon as she saw me, and I let Renni wave me off with that crooked grin of his even though I could tell he was scared ... Leathan—" She winces at the easy way e keeps saying her name. "—what if *she's* the one who killed him?"

No mortal could have done this, Yokuiv had said, but Leathan finds herself wondering, as she pries the hex from its bruising grip around her hips, if with the right kind of talisman arsenal, one *could* have. Had she caught the mortal merely stealing, or claiming a trophy? What better trophy, after all, than his beloved record player and the last demo he'd ever make?

"I'd have to find who she got the talismans from, see what else they gave her." It'd be someone who joined prior to the ceasefire. Newer recruits like her were never trained for battle, don't know what it takes to break through layers of contractual protections, or how to do it without drawing the attention of the entire outfit. "Why the fuck would a trouper give talismans this powerful to a mortal in the first place?"

"Greed, usually. You can get obscene amounts of energy bartering talismans to mortals—something about their attention being more focused, I'm not sure."

"Usually?" She twirls the purple pouch in her fingers, wondering how much energy a mortal would exude for it.

What she could earn if she could craft something this good—and she's confident she could. How long it would take her to get enough magic to break her curse then. And why she's never heard of anyone bartering talismans before now, if it's that lucrative.

"If she had one or two, maybe—but I saw the constructs, and the trail she left behind. She had at least a couple dozen. There's no way to pass that much energy off as legitimate earnings; not without parceling it out over several dozen performances. Most of it'd evanesce before you got your magic's worth out of it, or you'd get caught—and that's instant strike-out. Lihilim don't want their power getting into mortal hands." Eir lips tighten in a mirthless line. "Mortal hands not contractually bound to them, anyway."

"Someone thought it was worth the risk. But if not for the energy, then—" Leathan's fingers snag on a nasty knot of the hex, and she hisses in pain and frustration.

"Leathan—trust me, it goes better if someone else helps you out."

The way e reaches for her tells her e won't take no for an answer this time. "I'm done. See?"

Before Aqi can protest, she wrenches herself free with a final, inelegant slash of magic. Stabbing feeling rushes back into all her numbed extremities. Eyes watering—apparently this isn't damaging enough for her contractual protections to kick in, even if it hurts like all hells—she forces a nonchalant grin before fleeing from Aqi as quickly as the mortal had fled from her.

Eleven

The gym is a jungle of equipment: swings, hoops, trampolines, spinning target boards, wires, weights, knives, simplistic props. Whatever the performers need, their ringmaster makes sure it provides; yet somehow it can't rid itself of the pervasive smell of stale sweat and feet. Not that it doesn't try. Every morning it uses a different fragrance to attempt to cover the miasma that's sunk into it over centuries. Leathan, rubbing at the place between her ribs where her connection to Aqi wheedles into her like a splinter, takes a cautious sniff as she shoulders her way inside. Her nose wrinkles at the cloying mixture of pine needles and thyme.

After her failed capture of the mortal and the time she spent freeing the constructs—they may not be human anymore, but the way they writhed and struggled sure as hells read like human pain to her—she's disappointed but unsurprised the rest of the performers are already here. Many are in costume. The ones who aren't keep fiddling with their compacts. Low whispers vacillate between grief over Renni and anxiety about Yokuiv's absence and their postponed relocation.

Her ringmaster's charm unfurls in her chest, reaching in fifty directions at once. As she passes, troupers wave or offer tremulous smiles. She should stop and talk to them, find out if any of them gave Renni tea or bartered talismans to mortals—but she doesn't know if she can stand anyone else calling her by name the same way Aqi did. She needs a few minutes to brace herself first. A deep breath before the plunge.

Leathan beelines for her usual spot, a small island of scuffed blue mats by a mirrored wall away from the main part of the gym. As she steps around a tall basket of juggling equipment, she gets a jolt like an aftershock of the mortal's hex. Her island isn't deserted.

Dark hair piled in an untidy bun atop her head, sandy skin flushed and shining, the contortionist who'd found Renni bends her legs backwards over her shoulders into a careful balancing pose. Casallie—that's her name. It comes to Leathan as if she's always known.

Leathan hovers behind the basket, wondering if there's some other solitary nook she can shelter in, when the contortionist looks up and catches her gaze in the mirror.

Even knowing what to expect, Leathan still has to swallow her panic as illusory connection coils around the other trouper, transforming the blank exhaustion on Casallie's face into welcome. She pats the mat in an invitation Leathan cannot deny without jeopardizing Yokuiv's charm.

Leathan forces herself down on the edge of the mat and spreads her legs out into a spacious stretch. Sweat beads down her neck. Casallie looks at her. Is she supposed to say something?

"How'd you sleep?" Leathan signs haltingly. Like her weaves, she taught herself hand language over years of quiet observation.

Hazel eyes sagging, Casallie gives a languid shrug. "Couldn't, after …"

"Yeah—of course." Leathan grimaces, remembering the contortionist's scream, how she crashed out of Renni's trailer. "Must've been awful, finding him like that."

"No, it was fucking fantastic." Casallie inhales sharply, lower lip trembling. "Gods. I'm sorry. I shouldn't take it out on you."

"It's fine."

"It's not. I just can't stop thinking about—how if I'd gone back even a minute sooner, maybe I could've—I don't know. Done something." Petite as she is, Casallie seems even smaller, hunching her shoulders, curving into herself like she could disappear. It's a posture Leathan recognizes all too well. Without thinking, she reaches out to put a comforting hand on the contortionist's back.

No sooner does she start the gesture than she aborts it, grabbing her fingers with her other hand and rotating them down into a wrist opener with a bit too much force. Yokuiv's charm might deceive Casallie into thinking they're friends, but Leathan can't get caught up in the charade, too. "Don't beat yourself up over shitty timing."

"Why not?" Casallie digs the bottoms of her palms into her eyes. Her hands come away fissured with wet mascara. "He was always there for us when we needed him. Flitting around the Extravaganza like some burly fairy godmother." The apt description surprises a genuine guffaw out of Leathan. "But the one night he needs us to have *his* back, we fail him. *I* fail him."

Leathan squirms, adjusting the kerchief on her wrist, not liking how close Casallie's come to expressing thoughts she's been trying to ignore for the last twelve hours. "It's not like anyone could've known he was going to be murdered."

"Except his murderer."

A morbid chuckle catches in Leathan's throat. The corners of her eyes burn and prickle. She rubs at them, pretending to yawn so Casallie doesn't think she's crying. Which she's not. "Exactly. Unless that's you."

"No," she signs emphatically, "but the only reason I even went to his trailer last night was because I thought—"

Ruby flares in the contortionist's sandy cheeks. She rubs her palms on the side of her leggings with furious intensity. Leathan remembers the nervous way Casallie had composed herself at Renni's door, the speech she practiced. What *had* drawn her to seek Renni out alone, when she could've awaited him at the party? "Thought what?"

"I ..." Her fingers pluck at the stretchy black fabric along her thighs. She jumps at a burst of laughter from the main part of the gym, glaring over her shoulder at the offending troupers. Her fingers twist in nervous knots. "You won't tell anyone?"

Leathan covers her mouth with her compact, a gesture she's seen many of the others make. A mimicry of unlocking their jewel chest, which seems counterintuitive to swearing secrecy, but she supposes the intention matters more than the logic.

The contortionist glances around. No one's paying their little corner any mind, but she still leans closer so the pretzel of her body blocks her hands from any eyes that might wander their way. "After I got to the party, I noticed my bracelet was missing. I always make sure the clasp is secure, so I knew it couldn't have fallen off, and I definitely had it on when I went by Renni's. I'd held his hand so I could do a spin and show off my new party dress like I always do ..."

Leathan's brow furrows as she sees the shape of the thing Casallie's bending around. "You thought he swiped it."

"But of course he hadn't. It showed up—later. I just jumped to conclusions like an asshole when my trace led me towards his trailer."

"Your what?"

"My trace." A fat tear plops down Casallie's cheek. She rubs it angrily against the back of her calf. "No one's taught you that one yet?"

"No." Leathan doesn't bother to mention no one's taught her any spells at all. To her horror, the contortionist snaps her pale blue compact open. "Wait, don't waste the magic—"

"You'll understand better if I show you." Casallie ignores Leathan's protestations, weaving deliberate and slow with her chalked toes. Despite herself, Leathan follows hungrily along, committing to memory the order and different knots the contortionist uses. "Don't suppose you've misplaced anything recently?"

Leathan starts to say no, then remembers the tea pouch and the label torn off its back. A label that would bear the name of the shop it came from. She pulls it from her gym bag, watching the contortionist's face for any hint of recognition or dismay. Casallie doesn't seem like a murderer, but she was the only one who'd gone into Renni's trailer last night. Leathan can't rule anyone out.

Casallie only gives a confused laugh before laying the trace over the pouch. "Here I thought Renni was the tea fiend."

Leathan returns the laugh, though the mirth dies in her throat when she feels a warning flash of warmth deep in her chest. Somehow, over the course of a few minutes, she's gone from acting like a friend to dangerously close to becoming one. "I mean, you thought he was a thief, too."

The contortionist glances away. The fresh tears balancing on her lashes make Leathan regret the unkind jest, but she had to do *something* to stop their connection strengthening beyond the roots seeded by Yokuiv's charm.

They watch the trace settle in strained silence. Like a photograph developing in solution, a dull afterimage of the label appears. There's no text, only a simple map too blurry to read. Leathan sags with disappointment, but the contortionist swivels the pouch around like a dowsing rod until the trace brightens. Not by much, but now the map is legible enough Leathan can make out thick lines indicating cross-streets, complete with a star to mark the spot.

TWELVE

Training isn't over, but Leathan has a lead to follow now—
an actual lead, sparse and faint though it may be. Her
ringmaster's charm makes it harder than usual to make her
excuses, to slip away from Casallie and out of the gym,
given that everyone who catches sight of her wants to stop
her for small talk. Frazzled, she all but sprints to the storage
shed. She's desperate to escape beyond the Extravaganza
bounds and put half the city between her and the rest of the
troupe, even if it means another day with her pendant slung
around her neck, the cold glass clammy against her
breastbone.

Into the shed's dark depths stretch rows of shelving lined
with lacquered oak jewel boxes the size of Leathan's
clenched fist. Each houses a pendant like hers, though the
bits of curse sealed inside are of course different—not that

she's wondered about the other troupers' curses, let alone glimpsed any. Like people, no two are alike. The only thing curses share in common is the misery they inflict upon their victims. That, and they're supposedly impossible to break, which Leathan refuses to believe.

Yokuiv's charm stirring in her chest warns her she's not alone. She ducks into a shadowed corner near the entrance so whoever it is won't see her on their way out. No one spends more time here than it takes to unlock their jewel box and slip their pendant under their collar. The shed's a mausoleum, except instead of corpses entombed inside, it's curses. Curses that've been trapped for decades, marinating in their own warped power. Much scarier, and much more dangerous, than rotting flesh.

Thirty seconds pass. A minute. Leathan tugs on Renni's kerchief. She can't wait all morning for the other trouper to leave. Who knows how long Phenomenae will allow the Extravaganza to remain. How long she has to find Renni's killer.

Affixing her features in an expression of hurried purpose, which isn't difficult considering she's in all kinds of a rush, she strides forward. Hopefully whoever Yokuiv's charm is winding tight around takes the hint.

Bushy beard bowed as he braces his hands on either side of a shelf, Berhede whirls around so violently at her sudden appearance that he stumbles sideways, sending the shelf and its contents crashing to the concrete floor.

She suppresses a groan at the sensation of Yokuiv's charm settling in place, anchoring the big illusionist to her. "Didn't mean to scare you."

"Thought you were—" With a husky, awkward laugh, he scrubs his damp cheeks and beard on the rolled sleeves of his shirt, and bends to right the toppled shelf. He's in the same outfit he'd had on last night, but he looks so different to the raging trouper who'd rammed into her after banging on Renni's door, she almost hadn't noticed. "Thought you'd still be in training."

It's tempting to leave him to pick up the mess himself, to grab her pendant and go—but Leathan can't bring herself to be that much of an asshole, and kneels to help. There's a single jewel box, topsy-turvy among a sea of tea bags and candy tins and make-up pallets. She grabs the trinkets, the jewel box an uncomfortable presence in her peripheries. "What is all this?"

"Closure." Berhede is more gentle, more reverent with each item he replaces on the shelf. "Circusfolk don't leave bodies to bury. Our jewel boxes are the closest thing to a grave we get."

Which means that's Renni's jewel box, lying upside down out of sight. Strange, she thinks, to find Berhede of all troupers here, crying over a man he hated. Her fingers close around the last trinket someone left at Renni's ersatz tomb to say goodbye: a small heart of worn red silk, stitched along the edges with black trim, and dusty with long-since evanesced Extravaganza magic. She shoves it on the shelf with the rest. Who gives a spent love talisman to a dead man?

Berhede picks up Renni's jewel box, and the lid flops open. They both shriek louder than when Leathan found a cockroach on her pillow their first night in town. She flings her hands over her eyes; Berhede drops the jewel box with a clatter of heavy wood.

"It should be locked." Leathan swallows hard. "It shouldn't open without his compact."

"'The Agreement shall be rendered null and void when Undersigned Trouper's soul disincorporates from Undersigned Trouper's corporeal form.'" Every word sounds forced out around suppressed bile. "That means—"

"Right." Leathan knows the important bits of their contract well enough, but trust someone who's been in the Extravaganza for the better part of a century to have it sufficiently memorized to quote the lihilim legalese for *your contract ends when you die.* "No contract, no lock."

Both of them stay still as constructs. Berhede clears his throat. "Shouldn't leave it exposed."

"Mm," Leathan agrees. She doesn't move. No more contract may mean no more lock, but it doesn't mean no more pendant. Curses die when they do—learning that was a perverse relief, because at least if she can't find a way to break her curse in this life, it won't haunt her in the next—but until the magic evanesces after a couple weeks, pendants remain intact.

As do their contents.

Berhede clears his throat again. His day-old clothes rustle as he takes hesitant steps forward. Leathan presses her hands harder to her eyes to keep from imagining the illusionist tucking everything back into place.

"The *fuck?*" Berhede chokes. "It's—gone."

"What?" Leathan peeks through her fingers, ready to snap them shut again at the first glint of glass or gold filigree. There's nothing but Renni's jewel case, splayed on its side, the velvet lining spilling out like a fat tongue lolling over a slack jaw. Even glimpsing the empty guts of another trouper's jewel box, identical to her own, feels far too intimate. "It must've gotten flung somewhere. We'll find it."

Though she only learned the spell a quarter of an hour ago, Leathan ties every knot exactly as Casallie had demonstrated until she has a perfect reproduction of the contortionist's trace. Lightheaded and cold all over with sweat, she pinches the rounded edge of Renni's jewel box with forefinger and thumb, casts the weave over the lining, and braces for the sparkling outline of Renni's pendant to appear.

Nothing happens. Leathan's shoulders drop from where they'd ratcheted up to her ears. "What does that mean?"

The last of the color drains from Berhede's already ashen face. "It means it's *gone* gone."

"As in someone destroyed it?"

With a noncommittal grunt, Berhede takes the jewel box from Leathan's clammy palms and snaps the lid shut, thunking it down among the memorabilia on the shelf. "I better go prep my tent."

She knows an excuse when she hears one and can't blame the illusionist for being rattled. He strides out, leaving Leathan to rush to her jewel box in the back at last. Her compact morphs into a key when she brings it near the lid, and a matching lock appears among the arabesque designs. It takes her a few tries to fit the key into the slot, her mind still on Renni's empty jewel box.

No pendant. No lock.

And, she remembers, as hers clicks into place, no compact.

Did the killer steal his compact, unlock his jewel box, and destroy his pendant? But why destroy his pendant *and* him? The amount of power required for one act of violence, let alone both, boggles her mind.

The reddish-brown clippings of Leathan's curse tumble inside her pendant as she lifts it. They look dead and desiccated, but they're merely dormant, the curse suppressed by layers upon layers of her ringmaster's power. Maybe the killer didn't murder Renni themself after all. Maybe they destroyed Renni's pendant to release his curse and let it do the dirty work for them. Except rogue curses aren't that discerning, or that subtle.

Did they destroy it to cover their tracks? What evidence Renni's pendant could provide, Leathan has no idea—but she can't think of any reason to use that much magic except to hide something.

Grudgingly, she slips her pendant over her neck, tucking it away along with her questions.

It's time to start getting some answers.

THIRTEEN

There's the tiniest bit of resistance as Leathan passes the threshold between the liminal space in which the Extravaganza exists and human reality. It's so seamless an intersection, their mortal guests never notice they're stepping into a different world when they step into the circus. Not on a conscious level like the troupers do. Then again, mortals don't have their trapped curses hanging around their neck for the boundary to check for.

Mortals pack the downtown streets, a thick rainbow haze of energy winding over their heads. Nothing Leathan can legitimately absorb outside of her outfit and operating hours, but she likes to brush her awareness against it. With so many people around, unconcerned with anything but their own mundane day to day, it's comforting to feel part of something without risk of becoming attached.

She passes a group of young mortals, brown skin shining in the sunlight, two on guitars and one singing into a microphone. Energy eddies around the buskers, curiosity and interest and amusement. Like most mortals, they're unaware, but they must feel it, on some level—a rush of adrenaline or flush of satisfaction. All they'll get from the contact is a temporary high, an addiction that will keep them coming back again and again even if no one tosses a single coin into their open instrument cases. Most mortals know of magic what they know of space flight or war, of billionaires and famine. Those wonderful, terrible things exist, but not in any way meaningful for them.

It takes stopping in five different convenience stores to ask for directions and twenty minutes circling the block squinting at the trace before Leathan finds the tea shop. The entrance is concealed in a tiny staircase so narrow her eyes gloss over it until a fat black cat darts between two walls she could've sworn were adjoined.

She angles her body sideways to fit up the narrow passage, pursing her lips when she notices a poster advertising Phenomenae taped to the peeling paint at the mouth of the stairwell. Her eyes fix on the smudged shadow in the background, the faint outlines of a fox mask in the inky swirls. Zuna. How does she *always* find them?

She drags her focus away from the spy to the other troupers: a burly bronzed woman with blue-hot flame sprouting from her head, streaming from her mouth and nostrils; two smaller figures, one skinny and one fat, spinning gracefully on aerial hoops; and towering above them all, a woman in elaborate golden robes that accentuate the coppery undertones of her brown skin. Their ringmaster in human form. Abidine, the Circuit representative called her.

Four. Phenomenae's an outfit of *four*. No wonder Yokuiv was so incensed when Igmun insisted he negotiate with them. A spurt of spite makes Leathan tear the poster from the wall.

Even before she steps inside the tiny shop, her lungs fill with the rich scent of roasted leaves and herbs. The wooden door clatters open. Bells tinkle above her. Tea canisters and pouches like the one Leathan holds cram the walls, interspersed with ceramic cups worth a fortune in local mortal currency. Leathan keeps her movements gentle and close to her body as she picks her way through the small room.

The heavyset mortal organizing packets behind the till glances up, raising sparse eyebrows over her bifocals. Her deep brown skin is soft and wrinkled, dusted with darker sunspots. The cat loafs on a fur-coated cushion on the counter, blinking sleepy green eyes at Leathan.

The old woman sniffs the air once, twice, making the necklaces layered atop her apron clatter. "Another visitor from the circus."

A witch—she must be, to ken lihilim power when she smells it. Leathan holds up the pouch. "Like the one who bought this?" When the witch nods, Leathan's heart leaps into her mouth. "What did they look like?"

"Now, now." Grinning, the witch waggles a thick, knobby finger at her. "Can't get something for nothing."

Leathan bristles and takes a step back, angling the pocket containing her compact away. She's already been taken for a fool by one mortal with a modicum of arcane ability— hells, he could be friends with this witch for all Leathan knows—and she won't let that happen again.

"Relax, dear, it isn't magic I want. We have plenty of that to last us nine lifetimes, don't we?" The witch scratches two fingers under the cat's chin. The feline leans into her touch, pink nose scrunching, whiskers swiveling forward. "All I ask is a fair trade. You want a secret from me, then a secret you must give in exchange."

Leathan wishes the witch had asked for magic. She'd sooner empty her compact into the woman's coffers than give her what she wants. In the early days of Leathan's curse, before she learned better, it was always connections grown fat from shared secrets that took the longest for her curse to rip out of her. The ones that hurt the most.

Yet with one secret she might buy the identity of Renni's killer and clear both strikes from her record. She winds the blue and bronze kerchief around her wrist, thinking. The witch didn't specify what *kind* of secret. Maybe Leathan can give her a small one. One that means nothing. One whose grip will wither on its own, given enough time and distance for it to grow stale.

The witch crooks a finger to motion Leathan closer. Closer. Closer, until Leathan's leaning over the counter, the cat's rhythmic purrs rumbling up her arms, black fur and dust and roasted tea leaves and the witch's sweet perfume tickling her nose. Leathan puts her lips next to the woman's long-lobed ear, and whispers.

Fourteen

It isn't words that come out of Leathan's mouth, but a stream of shadows, of sensation and sound. Two figures manifest, facing off among a sea of darkened stalls. One is clearly Leathan, or clear enough; the other, hardly anything more than the masked blur from the Phenomenae advertisement she'd torn down. An intruder Leathan shouldn't have spoken to, even to tell them to leave; and as far as this witch gets to know, that's all that happened.

The tableau spins around the witch's head like a halo. With long nails she plucks the images into a glass jar.

Leathan feels at once lighter for the weight of speaking to the Phenomenae spy shared now between her and the mortal; and heavier, for the reedy connection twining between them. "You didn't say anything about storing it."

"Won't be a secret if I don't keep it, will it?" The witch holds the stoppered jar to her nose, squinting at the clouded contents swirling around inside. She gives a short harrumph and motions for Leathan to turn her head.

"I have nothing to put it in."

"Of course you do." She tugs playfully at the kerchief, tutting when Leathan jerks it out of her reach. "Unless you carry around a powerful protective talisman for sentimental reasons?"

Scowling, Leathan unties the fabric and drapes it over her palm before tilting one ear to the witch's wizened lips. Her low mutters warm Leathan's skin. An image—a memory—crackles to life in her mind, like watching television on the lowest volume, if the television were submerged in murky water, and her ears were plugged with wax and her eyes wrapped in gauze.

A figure stoops through the tea shop entrance, too fuzzy to make out in any detail beyond their looming height and girth. They give off the faintest sparks of magic. The witch's senses are too dull to recognize the specific signature of their lihilim ringmaster, but as with Leathan, she kens them as circusfolk with a sniff. Whoever it is notices the witch struggling with heavy boxes of new inventory, and, unbidden, moves to help her.

The witch watches them lift the boxes like they weigh nothing and teases that if they break any of her cups, they'll have to work for her for the next hundred years to pay it off.

They're so careful, so delicate, as if they expect her to make good on her threat. As if she has the power to overwrite the contract binding them to their lihilim ringmaster. She wishes wistfully she did. They'd make a handsome assistant.

Leathan struggles to discern the features the witch finds so attractive, but the shadows cling to the figure's face. Then they turn to ask the witch to craft a special tea to mask the bitterest of medicines, and into view comes a lovingly groomed beard.

Her mind immediately conjures Berhede. She imagines him the way she'd found him in the shed, shoulders stooped and cheeks damp from crying, wearing the same clothes as when he was shouting and pounding on Renni's door. So gentle one moment, so aggressive another—but does that make him capable of calculated murder?

Besides, Berhede isn't the only big bearded trouper in the Extravaganza. Without seeing more of the figure, she can't be entirely sure it's the illusionist, yet the witch's secret surrenders no further detail before it flickers and fades.

"That's it?" she growls. "You promised me a fair trade."

"You got what you paid for, dear." Mauve annoyance bubbles up from the old woman's shoulders as she shakes the jar containing Leathan's own murky secret. "I'm happy to provide further details if you have anything else to trade for them."

The cat yawns, stretches, and flips over to reveal a fluffy expanse of belly. A dangerous invitation gleams in its green eyes. Leathan glares at the witch and the cat both. She knows better than to fall for this trick.

"No." Leathan's fingers stray to her compact. She doesn't have the time or the magic—or the inclination—to force the witch to give her what she's owed, but the witch doesn't know that. "I'm done trading."

The witch explodes into laughter. The cat scrambles off the counter with a yowl and darts past a tattered curtain into the back room. "You're a recent recruit, aren't you? Post ceasefire."

Sky blue amusement crests off her and lashes against Leathan. She grinds her teeth against the sting. "I don't see how that matters."

"Because, dear, if you'd been around since the war, you'd have taken what you wanted without embarrassing yourself with empty threats." Still giggling, the witch pats the air in dismissal, following her feline past the curtain. "You won't harm me, and you won't trade me, so you might as well go."

Drenched in the witch's disdain, Leathan wraps the kerchief around the threadbare secret of the bearded trouper and storms from the tea shop in a hail of chiming bells. So tightly does she cling to her anger as she stomps down the narrow stairs, she nearly misses the whiff of sweet honeysuckle curling towards her. She slows, sharpening her senses. Kens the honeysuckle again, along with golden hour sun and the slide of soft down against skin.

Zuna.

No sooner does she think their name than they appear at the bottom step. She doesn't understand how—magic signatures are unique to ringmasters, not individual troupers—but she knew it would be them. The same way she spotted them in the poster. The same way she always knew where they were during a show.

Their slender body blocks the exit. They aren't in costume, though Leathan can't help feeling on edge. Perhaps she'd been tempting luck to mention their meeting to the witch, even in the vaguest of terms. But her luck doesn't need temptation to work against her. There must be some reason for the spy's presence. Are Phenomenae upset about the Extravaganza's refusal to relocate? Negotiations must still be ongoing, or Leathan would've felt the pull of Yokuiv's command to return. Maybe they decided to take matters into their own hands. No need to worry about violating the ceasefire now, when they can claim the

Extravaganza's done that already by remaining in the city past their scheduled run.

The tilt of Zuna's fox mask seems unsurprised, if not unperturbed, to see her. Did they ken Extravaganza magic and also know, somehow, it would be Leathan? "Hello, stranger."

"Come here often?" she deadpans.

Slowly, deliberately, Zuna pulls themself up a single step. "First time, actually."

"I wouldn't bother. The quality's subpar and the owner less than helpful. Save yourself the disappointment."

The designs on their mask shift in pensive patterns. "Perhaps there's somewhere else you could recommend."

"I could." Leathan forces herself down the steps until she's close enough to brace her forearms on either wall and lean over the spy. The calculated posture won't allow her to easily grab for her compact, implying they're too weak for her to need it. "But I don't see why I should."

Leathan doesn't miss the bob of the spy's throat as they swallow. "I can offer you information in return. About Renni."

Her prepared retort, tailored to brush them aside and out of her way, dies on her lips. They're bluffing. Trying to make themself seem useful so she doesn't attack them? No, they're nervous, not scared. It's more likely they're hoping to trick her into divulging some weakness or vulnerability they can exploit.

She should refuse on those grounds alone. But they did spend two months spying on the Extravaganza; it's not out of the realm of possibility they know something that could help identify Renni's killer. It's either take a chance on them, or spend the rest of the afternoon surreptitiously interrogating Berhede and every other bearded trouper with Yokuiv's charm tripping her up, making her feel things she shouldn't. She won't have that problem with Zuna. They aren't friends—will never—*can* never be friends.

"Fine," she says. "I know just the place."

FIFTEEN

The café Leathan leads Zuna to smells of fresh coffee and stale musk. Dark timber beams and plaster walls blush amber under soft light spilling from burnished iron sconces, and piano music lilts from unseen speakers. After the young server takes their order, Zuna leans their chin on one fist, their glittering eyes surveying the inner garden to their right before flicking back to Leathan. "I never would've found this place on my own. I'm so glad I ran into you."

She doesn't believe it was coincidence, not for one second, but the spy's trying to make her call their bullshit, to stall and distract from the reason they're here. "You promised me information."

"I was hoping you'd indulge me a few more pleasantries first." They slouch against the curved back of their seat. "But I understand. Renni is—he was one of a kind. I'm sorry."

"Not as sorry as you'd be if it was anyone else from the Extravaganza you ran into out here."

"Is that a threat, or a warning?"

Leathan shrugs. A little of both, maybe. "Most of them are convinced you're the one who murdered him."

"But you're not."

"Am I wrong?"

"If you were," they stage whisper, "I wouldn't correct you, would I?"

The server brings their order. Zuna presses the wide straw of their brown sugar boba tea to the lips brushed in bright red on their mask. Little black silhouettes of tapioca zoom up, and they sigh, contented. Leathan's urge to take the mask between her fingers and examine the spell's every knot and loop is so strong, her spoon shakes in her fist. She smears the heart-shaped ketchup on her omelet rice and takes a far bigger bite than she means to.

"If not me," they say, "who *do* you think killed your best friend?"

Leathan chokes on her hastily swallowed food. "Renni and I barely spoke—we weren't even acquaintances, let alone—"

A breeze rattles the latticed window beside her. Leathan jumps, hand jerking to her curse pendant, elbow flailing wide and knocking her iced yuzu soda right into Zuna's lap.

"Shit—*fuck*." Leathan unspools a thin thread of magic to vanish the soda soaking into the thighs of their linen trousers, but they laugh and lay a hand the color of rich red clay on hers to stop her weave. Leathan's skin sparks. She can't tell if it's from the spell snuffing out, or the softness of their fingers on her knuckles.

"It's all right." They dab at the stain with a wad of napkins. They're still holding her hand. Leathan flinches away, but the stubborn warmth of their touch lingers. She scrubs her hands on her towelette as if she could scour what just happened from existence.

"What I think doesn't matter," she sputters, wrenching the conversation back under her control. "We're not here to compare notes."

"I suppose not." Their chopsticks hover over a small ceramic dish of vivid pink pickled radish slices. At last deciding, they pick one and slide it into their muzzle. They chew, slow and deliberate, before continuing. "Remember that show your first week in? When a couple of you came close to falling short of quota?"

As if Leathan could forget their worst performance since she'd joined, though she'd spent the rest of the run trying. Renni had missed a cascading string of marks, marks she'd seen him hit with grace and ease a million times in training, marks he could've hit in his sleep. The audience recoiled with each of his missteps, energy dwindling to less than a trickle no matter how she or any of the others desperately attempted to entice them back into the show. It had felt like trying to claw her way up a cliff as it crumbled beneath her. "Everyone managed in the end."

"You certainly made sure of that."

Her snarl of a heart leaps into her throat. "I don't know what you're talking about."

"Relax," the spy soothes. "None of the others noticed you helping them, not that night or any other. You're very subtle, though I don't know why you go to such lengths to stop them knowing how much you care."

The bottom lurches out from under her. They'd been watching her far more closely than she thought, if they'd seen her redirecting energy when no one else ever had. "I don't care."

"Then why bother?"

"It's the right thing to do."

"You and I both know that's not the only reason."

They're stalling again, amusing themself in the meanwhile—but Leathan is an entertainer, not an unwitting toy. If the spy wants to play, it's going to be according to *her* rules. She drops her cutlery onto her half-full plate. "Fuck you if you're only going to mock me."

"I'm not—I swear I'm not." They don't touch her, but they sound so sincere, it halts her pushing back from the table the same as if they'd grabbed her, makes her forget for a split second she's not actually going to leave. "I'm trying to give you a compliment."

Leathan scoffs, crossing her arms to hide how much she's trembling. She's not sure if she's glad they fell for the ruse or not, or that whatever information they have for her—if any—is worth subjecting herself to their taunting. Compliment, indeed. "Give me the information you promised instead."

They look like they want to say something else, but sigh and rake their curls away from their mask. "That night, I overheard some trapeze artists arguing as they left the big top. Two of them were trying to get the other one to calm down. A big trouper with this brilliant red beard."

A thrill zips down Leathan's spine. There aren't many red-haired troupers with beards in the Extravaganza, and fewer still assigned to the big top. The village priest, the outraged uncle of one of the lovers, the forest witch who hides them, and—

Aqi.

She'd almost forgotten e wasn't always clean-shaven. E'd shaved so early in the run, and the change was so drastic, she can only picture Aqi as e'd been that morning—

dressed in costume, running eir hand along eir smooth jaw, scanning the backyard for a mortal wielding Extravaganza magic. "Funny you mention em … Who was e arguing with?"

The spy's mask twitches its ears. "A tall white woman who played one of the rain clouds, and a short Black man who was a butterfly."

Hard as it is to conjure what Aqi looked like before shaving, it's harder still to picture em and Vetsla and Te'ide fighting, or in fact doing anything but making out beneath Leathan's trailer window, grabbing and grasping like they need each other more than air. "What does a lovers' spat have to do with anything?"

"They were fighting about Renni. The one with the beard was ranting about how careless he'd been, how it's only a matter of time before he slips up again." Zuna reaches for another pickle, except there's none left. They set their chopsticks across the plate. "How e'd petition Yokuiv for the position emself before letting that happen."

Leathan leans back in her seat, stunned. No one *wants* to be star. She never understood why, always thought the extra magic made up for the extra responsibility and lack of freedom, until she glimpsed Renni stagger away from Yokuiv's office after the doomed performance, drained to dregs from whatever punishment he'd endured for failing to rescue the show. Renni'd caught her watching, and the crooked tooth grin he dredged up for her was so thin and haunted it churned her stomach. "E didn't mean it."

"E did. E was scared for eir lovers—they'd come close to their third strike that night. But they were dead set against em petitioning, of course. Not that I blame them. Your ringmaster's demanding of his stars."

"No more than any other." She's unsure whether it's true or not, but she can't let Zuna think her weak enough to let them imply ill of Yokuiv unchallenged. "Not that it matters. E never petitioned, or the entire Extravaganza would've been in an uproar."

"No. Eir lovers said they couldn't be with em if e went through with it, so e swore not to." Again those strange swirling patterns dance across Zuna's mask, so similar to wind tearing through leaves and twigs that Leathan's chest twinges. "But when someone's that desperate, it makes you wonder—what else would e do to protect the people e loves?"

Sixteen

A pair of elderly men at the other end of the café get up, chair legs scraping across the stone floor. Leathan chews her thumbnail, attention half on the mortals settling their bill at the register, half on the spy sitting across the table, their knee centimeters from touching hers. "You think petitioning to replace Renni as star would lose Aqi eir lovers, but committing *murder* wouldn't?"

"Not if they never found out."

"That's a pretty big if."

"Look, I'm not the detective here. All I can do is provide the clues; you're the one who has to make sense of them."

Worrying the knot of the kerchief at her hip, Leathan strings the disparate threads together in her head the same exploratory way she allows before-her to create spells from scratch: Aqi blames Renni for eir lovers nearly striking out, but eir lovers don't want em petitioning to be star, so e decides to kill Renni instead—goes to the tea shop, shaves to conceal eir identity in case anyone goes looking—and, what, hopes whoever Yokuiv names star next doesn't mess up as badly? Or worse, more likely; there's no one in the Extravaganza who'd make a better star than Renni even on a bad day, Aqi included.

Though if e was going to petition, e must think e *would* do better. Would Aqi keep killing stars who don't perform to eir standards, until eirs is the name Yokuiv puts in the marquee? It's too loose a weave for her liking, riddled with gaps and frayed ends, but no less threadbare than an obsessed stalker taking things too far, or an illusionist with a chip on his shoulder ending a years-long grudge once and for all.

"Why's it funny?"

Leathan blinks at the spy, helping themself to her cooling omelet rice. "*Excuse* you!"

"What? You weren't touching it, and I can't stand the thought of wasting good food." On their mask, a tiny, velvety tongue peeks out from between sharp teeth. "You said it was funny I mentioned em."

She snatches her food back, wiping the spoon with a napkin in case the mask's magic only made it *seem* like the silverware never touched the spy's actual lips. It gives her time to decide how to explain. Walking this line—honest enough to get useful information in response, but not enough the spy gets the wrong idea about the Extravaganza's strength—feels like tightroping in shoes two sizes too big. "E's the one who found me this morning after I chased a stalker out of our backyard."

Behind their mask, the spy's black-lined eyes go wide. As Leathan scarfs the rest of her meal, if only to prevent Zuna scavenging from her plate again, she recounts finding the mortal woman coming out of Renni's trailer. She doesn't mention she'd seen the mortal before, loitering near the storage shed, which means she'd stayed in their circus undetected all night after closing; or that the mortal had disarmed half a dozen constructs and broken into Renni's trailer to steal his record player.

"I would've caught her, if one of her talismans hadn't landed a lucky hit." She smacks the inert purple pouch against the tip of Zuna's snout, taking immense satisfaction from their startled yelp. "She fled past the threshold a few seconds before Aqi showed up. When I told em it was a mortal, e knew who I meant. Apparently she'd been stalking Renni the whole run. She even cornered him the other night and wouldn't leave him alone until Aqi intervened."

"Renni always did put other people's needs before his own. Even when he shouldn't."

Like how he'd nearly missed his cue last night in case Leathan needed his help. *More* of his help. She jars as she bites down on a piece of grit in the rice. Eyes watering, she pushes her plate away from her. Now she's made it obvious she's finished with her meal, she doesn't care if Zuna steals the scraps.

They don't, too busy examining the spent talisman. "This was crafted out of Extravaganza magic."

"And those keen observation skills are why your ringmaster made you her spy."

"Abidine doesn't squander the strengths of her troupers, unlike some."

Another barb meant for Yokuiv. Leathan levels a flat stare at the spy to make it clear she's letting their attack go unanswered because it's not worth responding to, rather than her not understanding enough to counter. "I should get back. Follow up with Aqi. Something tells me e knows which trouper traded her those talismans."

"Wait." Zuna hurries after her as she slaps more than enough local mortal tender down at the till to cover both of their meals before striding out of the sliding doors. From behind her, she hears the spy click their tongue. "Lunch was supposed to be my treat. Leathan, *wait*—are you sure it was a trouper?"

Leathan slows and wipes sweat from beneath her bangs. Despite the thick cloud cover, or perhaps because of the oppressive threat of rain making everything moist and sticky, it's too hot to be moving fast. "Who else would she have gotten them from?"

"Any mortal with arcane ability and knowledge of the craft."

"Knowledge is one thing, but it's not like anyone would have that much Extravaganza mag—" Leathan stops. Her omelet rice roils in her stomach. She knows of one mortal who *would*:

That cheat of a mystic.

Zuna's ears perk in excitement when Leathan spins on her heel. "Where are we going?"

She doesn't waste time answering or trying to stop the spy following her. Either they'll get bored and wander off on their own, or they won't. It's all the same to Leathan, as long as they stay out of her way.

They do get bored once it becomes apparent they can't wheedle her into conversation, but never show any inclination of abandoning her. Every now and then they go fuzzy, as if fading into the very shadows themselves, but Leathan never loses sight of them.

The thick purple shade of the mystic's parlor is drawn. The handwritten sign inside the window is scrawled with

CONSULTATION IN PROGRESS, which Leathan now knows means there's another gullible mark in there getting scammed out of their life savings for nothing but empty promises. Even if she didn't, the muffled voice within speaking of "paying the tolls to the other side" would tell her the same thing.

As she squares herself on the grimy welcome mat, she notices the capsule machine to the left, the one she pulled the twin kitties from, has been refilled with some other series of trinket. It gives her an odd pang to think they were taken away the same day as Renni. She sees him cup the keychains in hand, hears him coo over their sparkling little forms.

Hot tears sear her eyes. If this mystic is the one who made those talismans, and the mortal used them to kill Renni, then it's Leathan's fault he's dead.

Behind her, Zuna asks, "Everything all right?"

"It will be," she mutters, and slams the door open.

Seventeen

There are screams and plumes of green and orange. Two mortals cower at a low square table in the middle of the parlor. To the young one trembling on the very cushion Leathan herself had perched upon yesterday, she says, soft as thistles, "Get out."

She angles herself to let the young mortal flee past in a streak of chartreuse, her glare frozen on the older one. The one she's here for.

Cloaked in a clashing riot of confusion and fear, the mystic who scammed her out of a decade's worth of magic stares up at her. Though it's been less than a day since he last saw her, no recognition lights in his face. Heat rises in Leathan's. She expected him to remember her, but why would he? To him, people like her and that young mortal aren't worth noticing beyond what he can exploit out of them.

It's better he has no idea who she is. This way, her naiveté won't be outed to Zuna. The spy's likely already gleaned someone from the Extravaganza was swindled here, but they don't need to know it was her.

At his breast the mystic clutches a beaten bronze bowl sloshing with milky liquid, an indistinct image of a shadowy figure shivering on its rippling surface. Tatty and weakly woven from mortal magic though it is, Leathan recognizes the conjuring. It's similar to one in rotation at the Extravaganza's own Tent of Illusions, in which magic is melded with memory to summon a projection of whoever someone in the crowd is thinking about.

"A cheat *and* a cheapskate." Leathan stalks forward. The bowl clatters to the carpeted floor as the mystic collapses backwards, scuttling away until he collides with a wobbly wooden cabinet. Dread flares in her as she kens Extravaganza magic nearby, hints of vanilla mingling with the mystic's incense and the soft tingle of electricity jumping between the little hairs on her arms. It's too faint to tell how much there is, or what shape it might be in, but that gives her little comfort. "That poor kid not worth tricking with the good stuff?"

"You can't—" The dry squeak in his voice and the twitch of his thick upper lip weaken his outrage. "You can't barge in here—I've read the ceasefire, there are *rules* now, there are *protocols*—"

"What do the rules say about stealing lihilim magic?" Zuna skips their fingers over shelves and opens drawers, searching, probing. Leathan shoots them a dubious glance, wary of whatever it is the spy hopes to gain by involving themself.

"Steal?" the mystic stammers.

"Something about being turned into a dung beetle, I'm pretty sure," says Leathan.

"That's right." The maw of Zuna's mask stretches wide in unmistakable glee. They pluck a flower out of a narrow vase in the corner, dragging the puff of tiny purple blossoms along one cheek. "I thought cockroach, but that's for lying to a representative of the Greater Circuit."

"Easy mistake."

"I never," whimpers the mystic. He props himself up on one bony elbow, eyes careening between Leathan and Zuna so fast she doesn't know how he isn't making himself dizzy. "I don't know what you're talking ab—"

"A trouper came to you recently." It takes all her self-control not to glance to Zuna again, to see if they caught the hitch in her voice, the bend in the truth. "Return to me what you took from her."

"I didn't *take*—" He yowls and flings his arm over his face as Leathan slams her palm against the cabinet hard enough to make its insides rattle.

"Do you want to find out what lying to *me* gets you turned into?" Magic sparks like a blizzard of fireworks around her clenched fist, and the parlor fills with the scent of Extravaganza power and charring cabinet wood. She learned at the tea shop not to make empty threats, and so she weaves, not sure what it will be, what it will do, because she never looks too closely while before-her works.

"I—" The mystic's unblinking eyes reflect her weave in distorted detail as the spell takes its menacing shape between her hands. His tongue darts out once, twice to wet his lips. "I've done nothing wrong. She paid me for services rendered. That's called a transaction."

"If you'd done what she asked," Leathan hisses, jaw aching from how hard she's clenching her teeth. "But you didn't—in fact, you knew you couldn't, and yet you dangled false hope in front of her anyway. That's called a *scam*."

Scoffing with forced gravitas, the mystic squares his shoulders and digs his heels into the carpet to sit up straight—as straight as he can, still wedged between Leathan's legs and the cabinet. "Sounds more like buyer's remorse to me."

With a snarl, Leathan strikes the cabinet again. It jars her hold on the weave and makes the threads tangle, but before she can salvage the spell, there comes a dull *sproing* of a catch releasing, and a small compartment pops open on the far side of the cabinet in a confetti of dust. At her feet, the mystic gulps.

She lets the magic sink back into her compact; no need to waste it now. Inside the compartment sits a golden coin, redolent of vanilla and petrichor, shimmering bright as lightning. Her ringmaster's signature crackles over her skin when she plucks the talisman out. The weave—for prosperity—is simple but skilled, strong enough to last years before effervescing. Leathan turns it over in clammy fingers. Whoever crafted this could've easily crafted the talismans Renni's stalker had, and the magic is fresh enough it could've come from what she'd given the mystic yesterday.

"Is this what you did with it?" She shoves the coin in the mystic's face. He recoils, though his gaze remains locked on the talisman, his hands curling and uncurling as if he's restraining himself from snatching it out of her grasp. "You took more than this. How many of these did you make? Where are the rest?"

"What I did or didn't do with my legitimate earnings is none of your business," he growls. "Your friend can't complain about the quality of my service when she didn't give me what I needed to do my job."

It'd be so easy to pick up this scrawny man by his collar and throw him across the room, but harming a mortal, even one who so clearly deserves it, is grounds for another strike she can't afford. Not until Yokuiv wipes her record clean. Fighting the impulse, Leathan chokes out, "She gave you almost everything."

"Not her cooperation." The mystic lifts his chin, defiant, indignant. "I suppose when she complained of how I 'scammed' her, she left out how she fought my efforts the entire time. If she'd worked with me instead of against me, I might've stood a chance of breaking through the enchantment on her memory."

Leathan's mouth opens and closes as she fights to respond to his nonsense. Fought him? She should have, but she just sat there and sweated and let him glut himself on her magic. "She didn't come here to cure her amnesia—and she's not enchanted, she's *cursed*. I thought you were a con, but it turns out you're just inept if you can't tell one from the other."

"I know the fucking difference." The mystic jabs two fingers to his sternum. "She pointed right here and said, *I want you to break this*, and when I looked in her heart I saw the enchantment—not a curse, an *enchantment*—a tricky little web gumming up everything from about two decades ago—"

This time Leathan recoils. She never told him *when* she was cursed. But that doesn't mean there's an enchantment on her, whatever the mystic claims—her *curse* severed her, split her into *before* and *after*. He's spinning this tale of some sort of tragic misunderstanding to validate his claim to her magic, digging into the fabrication because he's cornered. That's all.

Yet as the mystic explains to her like he would a child things she already knows about how to tell a curse from an enchantment from a charm, she can't help but check. She focuses her senses inward, peers more closely at the ruins of her heart than she has in—well, in twenty years.

She probes at her heart as carefully as she did the poison in Renni's tea, poring over it for as long as she can bear the pain. It's only when she forces herself to keep looking past those limits, she finally kens it: a gleaming gossamer net of mortal magic strung up over the darkened half of her heart, pulsing in sync with its beat.

"Don't." The mystic, suddenly frantic, leverages himself against the cabinet into a low crouch, palms extended towards her in supplication. She looks down; she's drawn magic from her compact again, and her knuckles have gone white around the coin. The pure power causes the weave to warp and the metal to crack, but she can't feel it in her hand. She can't feel anything.

"You have plenty of magic to make another," she says, and crushes the talisman into dust.

Hissing like a wild animal, the mystic lunges for her. The low table breaks under their combined weight, as does Leathan's right wrist when she lands on it wrong. The mystic is yelling. Leathan hardly hears him over the snap and pop of her contractual protections healing her bones, the frantic scuffling of their bodies as he bats her good hand away from her compact. "Not like that one, but you knew that already, knew I can't even replace it with him gone—"

Zuna is there, quick as a shadow, smacking the jinx out of the mystic's grip before Leathan even realizes he's made a weave. They wrench him up and wrap a lithe spell around him head to toe, binding him to the wall. He writhes in the cocoon of Phenomenae power as Leathan gets to her feet, steadied by the spy's gentle touch.

"Leave him with me," they murmur, picking splinters from her clothes, her hair and skin. "I'll get the truth out of him. You get some air."

Too numb to argue, too breathless to speak, Leathan can do nothing but nod.

Eighteen

Half a block down the alley from the mystic's parlor, Leathan paces in front of a stone bench. She tried to sit, at first, only to leap to her feet seconds later. Something hot and wet and salty rolls off her face. Bile stings the back of her throat. Arms wrapped tight around her middle, fingers of her freshly healed right hand worrying the knot of Renni's kerchief, she walks the same five feet of pavement over and over and over.

An enchantment. An *enchantment* on her heart she'd never noticed, until some two-bit con man pointed it out to her on accident. An enchantment is the reason she can't remember the first half of her life, not her curse like she always thought. But why wouldn't she have assumed her curse was to blame, when her memory sheers off like a cliff before the first time it took her?

The timing is too perfect to be coincidence. Was whoever cursed her the same one who enchanted her? But why curse her *and* enchant her? It's as pointless as punching someone after slicing off their head.

Whoever did this must've wanted to make good and fucking sure Leathan didn't remember anything before they cursed her. Did they know each other? Were they afraid she'd seek revenge?

Without the enchantment in place, would she remember something that would break her curse?

Leathan draws several bracing breaths before diving her awareness back to the place inside her where she kenned the magic. It's so easy to find, now that she's willing to delve deep enough, to brave the pain long enough, to look.

And oh, how it hurts even to look. Like taking a scalpel to a migraine. Like biting down on iced nails. She doesn't actually grit her teeth and squint, but that's what it feels like she has to do to even glimpse this enchantment's repellent gleam, before it surges forward and body slams her out of her own mind.

She sinks onto the bench, panting, holding her soaked face in trembling hands. No wonder the mystic thought she was fighting him, but even if she'd known to help, it wouldn't have made a difference. It's strong—stronger than any mortal magic Leathan's encountered before, except, perhaps, her curse.

One day, she'll find a way to break both.

Phenomenae magic glides along her skin. She glances up as Zuna takes a seat on the bench beside her.

"It wasn't your friend's magic in those talismans," they say.

Leathan's lips twist. They must know, after what happened in there, that it wasn't her "friend" the mystic had scammed. "You're sure?"

"Positive. He's part of some wider group. Wouldn't specify the scope, only that they all send whatever magic they squeeze out of circusfolk to a main headquarters somewhere." They realize they're still holding the purple flower they took from the mystic's vase, and toss it over their shoulder with a sigh. "Wouldn't specify where that is, either, of course, but the important thing is they don't craft talismans."

Relief sprouts and withers. "Where'd the one in the cabinet come from?"

"He bought it from a wandering artisan to help his business along. Apparently—" The spy gives Leathan a wry look. "—he was falling short of his monthly quotas."

She wants to laugh at the irony, but the mirth dies in her throat. It might not have been her magic powering the talismans, but it's obvious there's a leak in her outfit. Whoever crafted that coin can tell her where. "I have to find that artisan."

The spy steps in front of her when she stands, an apologetic grimace on their mask. "He said they've already left, didn't mention where they were headed next."

Great. That's all her leads at a dead end. She's out of options except to return to the Extravaganza and subject herself to Yokuiv's charm.

"There's nothing else you can tell me?" She hopes she doesn't sound as desperate as she feels. The asphalt reflects hot sun into her eyes. She wipes sweat from her brow and wonders, between their mask and all those layers of clothes, how Zuna can stand there looking so cool and unbothered. "Nothing else you saw over two months of spying on us that gave you pause?"

"There is." They shift closer, their body shading her. "You."

Leathan's back hits the plaster wall. She wasn't even aware of moving. She's used to their gaze lingering on her for hours at a time—but from a distance. This is different from when they sat hundreds of meters away, one in a crowd of thousands, watching her from across the big top while she spun through the comfort of choreographed movement, raw mortal energy thrumming through her every molecule making her feel invincible. Invulnerable.

They're toying with her again. They must be. Leathan tries to snort, but it comes out more of a strangled whimper. "You aren't a very good spy."

"Utterly useless." They toss her a wink. "In my defense, I didn't anticipate needing to help you solve a murder, or I'd have made more of an effort to pay attention to the others."

Whatever retort she's scrambling for escapes her when Yokuiv's presence sparks to life in her mind. The summons back to the Extravaganza is impatient and displeased; not with her, but it still makes her wince. Things must not have gone well at the negotiations—and here she is, bandying words with his enemy's spy when she should be hunting his star's killer.

"I have to go."

Zuna's glittering brown eyes anchor her to the spot as they search her face. She's not sure what they're looking for, or what they're hoping to find. "There's another option."

They press a slip of paper into her hand, tingling with Phenomenae magic. Her instinct should be to drop it, burn it, tear it up—who knows what sort of hex or jinx could be woven into its fibers—but instead, Leathan looks down. It's an old-fashioned ticket, pulpy paper stamped with ADMIT ONE in bright red ink.

"You want me to come to Phenomenae?" A star-shaped hole punched out of one corner looms large in her vision. "As your guest? I might as well paint a target on my back."

"That ticket guarantees your safety. Not that any of us would hurt you to begin with. Hells, your magic is so strong, none of us could."

One enemy Leathan can easily take—but not an entire outfit, ringmaster and all; not in their own circus. Not even one as small and weak as Phenomenae. She holds the ticket out to Zuna like it's a deadly viper about to strike. "Even if I didn't have Renni's murderer to find—"

"Please." They fold their hands around hers, sandwiching the rough paper against her palm. Phenomenae magic drifts warm and gentle between their fingers. Leathan should pull away, but she doesn't. Her fingers are so cold despite the heat of the afternoon. "Come with me. There are things I want to tell you—show you—that I can't outside my outfit. I swear on my pendant, if anyone does try to hurt you, I'll protect you myself."

A sensation explodes within her like hundreds of roots sprouting from her chest, reaching, straining across the scant centimeters of space between her and Zuna. It feels like magic, but their hands are devoid of power, their compact shut tight.

Besides, Leathan knows it's no spell.

It's connection. The kind she hasn't felt since the last time her curse took her, changed her, left her bloodied and dying at the edge of the world. True, real, razor-edged, soul-baring, heart-flaying connection.

Leathan doesn't know if it's because she's trembling so hard, but she swears she feels her curse pendant jitter and jerk around her neck. Like the clippings inside can sense this bond blossoming, an entire garden sprouting from arid soil.

This wasn't supposed to happen. Zuna was—is—a stranger. An enemy. They were supposed to be *safe*.

"Leathan."

Performing for them night after night must have eroded her common sense. What was she thinking, sharing a meal with them, letting them tag along to the mystic? Now they know how naive she is—and can guess what little magic she has left in her compact. That's why they want her to come to their outfit, so they can finish her off in the safety of their own territory. She needs to get out of here, to where they can't hurt her—

"Leathan—"

She runs.

"Leathan, wait!"

She doesn't look to see if they're giving chase. She weaves a spell to lengthen her strides, to shorten the streets—using far more magic than she needs in her haste. It's wasteful, but she needs to put as much distance between her and Zuna as fast as possible. Every step away from them is harder than the last. Without magic to help her, she might go back.

And she can't let herself get any more attached than she already has.

Nineteen

Despite it being hours past when the Extravaganza opens its gates, there are no mortals weaving their way through the labyrinthine paths towards the big top; no jugglers or stilt walkers ambling through the crowd; no whiff of cotton candy or steamed buns in the air. The only sounds are the desperate scream of cicadas in the sprawling maples, indistinct droning of fairground troupers half-heartedly prepping their stalls or sideshows for whenever and wherever the outfit opens next—and gravel snap-crackling beneath Leathan's feet.

The storage shed construct looks anywhere but at her as it steps aside to allow her access. Its attempt at giving her privacy is sweet. She wonders if that's spelled into its behavior, or if it's retained some of sense of social cues from its long-ago human life. Or if she's just projecting.

She sandwiches the crumpled Phenomenae ticket under her curse pendant in its velvet bed. She should throw it away, because it's contraband, and because she's never, ever stepping foot in Zuna's outfit; but she tried to toss it at a convenience store once she was sure she'd put enough distance between them, and couldn't. Another Phenomenae advertisement was taped in the window above the garbage can, and as she held the ticket over the pile of refuse, all she could do was stare at the poster. At the smudged shadow in the background, and the faint outlines of a fox mask staring right back.

Nothing else you saw over two months of spying on us that gave you pause?

There is. You.

Before-her stirred, then, urging Leathan for some unfathomable reason to keep the ticket. Crushing it in her fist, she turned from the poster with a growl and made no more detours on her way back to the Extravaganza.

If before-her insists she keep a scrap of paper that could earn her a third strike, then beneath her curse pendant is the only place it'll be protected from prying eyes. Unless someone steals her compact like they stole Renni's, though she figures if she's ever that fucked, a third strike will be the least of her concerns.

Ticket and pendant stashed, Leathan speed-walks to Yokuiv's office, his summons a gentle drumming of fingers in her head. The backyard's deserted until she gets to the park. She doesn't know why they call it the park; it's just an empty swath of tamped-down dirt where the paths to the other parts of the Extravaganza converge. But it's far from empty now. Dozens of troupers swarm the space, charming paper lanterns to float in mid-air, unfolding tables and chairs and canopies, arranging garlands of multicolored flowers.

It barely bothers her this time when Yokuiv's charm reaches out. Voices and hands lift in greeting. Most of them get the hint she's in a hurry, but as she heads towards their ringmaster's office, a light touch brushes her shoulder. "That's the last place you want to be right now."

Leathan looks up into the angular face of one of the knife throwers—Shieng, a head taller than her, dressed in black lace and ribbon, holding a tangle of star-shaped string lights. "Because he's pissed?"

"He was pissed last night. Now, he's …" Shieng pauses, picks at the lights as she searches for the word. The chipped polish on her short nails gleams like an oil slick. After a couple of fruitless seconds, she shrugs. "He's like he was this one time, before the ceasefire, when another outfit was encroaching on our turf. He sent us to deal with them. It was a long battle, and ugly, like they always were."

No one's ever spoken to Leathan about the war. Then again, she's never asked.

"We won." The knife thrower's dark green eyes go flat and dazed as if remembering anything but a victory. "Rounded up the surviving troupers for Yokuiv to inspect. One punched this gnarly hex square into his face. Blasted us all onto our asses. Knocked some of the others out. Wish it would've knocked me out, too, but I was lucid enough to—to watch. That hex didn't do shit to Yokuiv. He just laughed, then peeled that poor fuck's soul right out of their body and swallowed it down."

Leathan puts a hand to her throat, bile rising in her gullet. "That's a war crime."

"No shit, Leathan." The knife thrower lets out a mirthless laugh. "Didn't you ever wonder how the Extravaganza ended up so much more powerful than the other outfits?"

The question is so abrupt it takes Leathan a moment to register it's even been asked. "Because he has a knack for finding cursed mortals to recruit?"

Shieng makes a flat buzzer noise, then flicks a glance towards Yokuiv's office and motions Leathan closer. Close enough Leathan makes out the faint, jagged scar along one of her cheeks. "Lots of energy builds up in a mortal soul when it's stuck in an immortal body for decades. Makes what we earn on a good night look like peanuts in comparison. Kind of makes you wonder why more ringmasters didn't gorge their way to strength like he did, war crime or no, but I guess most humans don't go around committing mass murder, either, so—"

Shieng keeps musing on lihilim morality, but Leathan can't focus enough to listen. How many souls must Yokuiv have consumed to become as powerful as he is? Dozens? Hundreds? The thought makes her want to throw up. Then a worse realization strikes her. "He's still a ringmaster. The Circuit let him get away with it."

"Part of the bargain they struck so he'd sign the ceasefire. He was the last hold-out—hey, fuck, you all right?" Aghast, Shieng puts a steadying hand on her arm.

"Yeah." She extricates herself with a smile Renni would've been proud of. "Duly noted: don't fuck with our ringmaster or he'll eat you alive. Literally."

"I mean, not anymore. The Circuit couldn't prosecute him for what he did during the war, but they made damn sure to make it clear in the ceasefire lihilim can't go around consuming our souls without major consequences. Still, he doesn't need to rip your soul out of your body to make you wish you hadn't bothered him when he's this—wrathful. That's the word. Wrathful."

That, at least, Leathan doesn't need to be told. She thinks back to the doomed show at the start of their run; to Renni, limping his way through the backyard, a husk of himself. But she can't ignore Yokuiv's summons. The punishment for that would be worse than whatever he'll do to her when he hears just how little she's managed to progress the investigation in his absence.

She trudges off down the path to the canteen, opting to take a detour rather than explain why she'd still head towards their ringmaster's office after being warned against it. Shieng calls after her. "Don't ditch out tonight."

Talking about how the Extravaganza grew fat on war conquest in one breath and then festivities in another makes her head spin. Leathan lets out an awkward laugh. "Didn't we just have a party?"

"Not like this one." Squinting at her target with a practiced eye, Shieng throws up a loop of lights around the metal frame of the canopy. "This one's for Renni."

ᴛWENTY

When the construct admits her into Yokuiv's office, Leathan lingers at the threshold. She doesn't move, doesn't breathe, clinging to the moment before her ringmaster acknowledges she's arrived. He's reclined in his chair, embroidered cloak draped luxuriously over the back, swiveled away from the door and surveying his circus outside the window with half-lidded eyes. One hand swirls a coupe three-quarters full of a cloudy concoction redolent of anise seed and cloves; upon the other he pillows an angular cheek.

He's back in the mortal guise she's accustomed to: skin no longer glowing, nails clipped, wings vanished, the aura of sheer desire diminished. Leathan wishes she could take it as a good sign, but she can't read his posture as anything but the ease of a predator biding his time.

He lolls his head to the side and, without looking away from the window, murmurs, "I hope your day went better than mine."

Does a gentle threat underpin those words, or is she on edge after that whispered conversation with Shieng? She wants to ask about what happened at the negotiations, wants to know if they're being forced to relocate or allowed to stay, wants *something* to help her judge her day against his. But demanding information from her ringmaster seems ill-advised. "It was—eventful."

He chuckles. One thin eyebrow cuts into his forehead when he sees her hovering at the door, and he beckons her closer with a flick of a finger. Trying not to gulp, she stands in front of his desk, not presuming to take the chair opposite him. He hasn't offered. "Indeed. My constructs informed me of the mortal trespasser. They were very grateful you took the time to free them from her hex."

Heat creeps into her cheeks. She knew constructs were capable of communicating with their ringmaster. She didn't know they were capable of feeling—well, anything, let alone gratitude. "I didn't want to leave Renni's trailer unprotected."

Yokuiv's blue eyes glitter, with mirth or derision, Leathan can't tell. Does he think her weak for the unnecessary compassion? Is he angry she let the mortal escape? "They mentioned she stole something."

"His record player."

"His—record player." Her ringmaster repeats the words as if he's never heard of such a device. "So much effort for something so inconsequential."

"It wasn't." Shit—why is she arguing with him? Her mouth goes dry, and she hurries to explain, careful to keep her tone polite. "Not to her. She was stalking Renni our whole run, probably wanted something special of his. It had one of his demos on it. The last one he ever recorded."

"Is that so." He doesn't seem convinced, but lets it drop. "Were you able to determine the source of her talismans?"

"I found a local mystic in possession of a similarly crafted talisman. He claimed it was from a wandering artisan who's already left the city."

"How convenient." Yokuiv must be able to see the lies. The empty spaces she's left around the fact she found the mystic because she'd been scammed, that she learned about the wandering artisan thanks to Zuna. "Is that why you spent most of the day outside my outfit?"

Not doing as he'd instructed her to do and speak to the others, he means. Leathan clasps her hands behind her back to hide how they're shaking. "No, I—I went to training, and from there figured out where the killer bought the tea. When

I went to the shed so I could go look for the shop, Berhede was there, and I startled him into knocking a shelf over. Renni's jewel box fell, and when Berhede picked it up, the lid flopped open, and—it was empty. I cast a trace, but that didn't reveal anything. I think—I think the killer destroyed it, but I don't understand why."

Expression unreadable, Yokuiv tilts his drink to his lips, pausing for a long moment before setting the tumbler down on the coaster without ever taking a sip. "Were there any more delays on your way to the tea shop?"

Leathan shakes her head and, as she explains about trading secrets with the witch for the identity of the trouper who bought the tea, unpicks the kerchief and the memory it holds from where she'd tied it around her belt loop—or tries to. The fabric keeps slipping from her fingers so she can't get a good enough grip to work the knot free. She'd tied it securely, but not *that* securely. Fidgeting with the kerchief throughout the day must have tightened it.

Gaze expectant and unwavering, her ringmaster watches in taught silence. She's about to rip the belt loop from her skirt in desperation when the knot relents at last. Holding back a sigh of relief, she sets the kerchief on the desk. The fabric, so slippery moments before, now seems to static-cling to her fingers.

Her ringmaster hums as he unbundles the secret. "Quite the impressive protective charm you wove into this."

"It's actually Renni's work."

"Is it?" Yokuiv draws a corner of the kerchief between his fingers. "A precious gift. You two were closer than I assumed."

With a half-hearted shrug, she glances out the window to the big top, to the blank, stagnant marquee curved around its peak. Strange, for it not to be moving, for it to no longer bear Renni's name in glowing pastels. "He only gave it to me because he took his responsibilities too seriously."

"I always did admire how—diligently—he strove to keep his companions safe." The kerchief wilts away under Yokuiv's touch, revealing a small, shimmering orb. He scoops it out with the knife edge of his palm; the orb crumbles, shadow and sensation and sound issuing from the cracks to dance around his crown.

"It's not very detailed," she says, to temper his expectations as the figure of the bearded trouper appears. Yokuiv leans forward, lithe fingers steepled at his mouth. "I know it's not much to go by, but—"

"On the contrary." To Leathan's surprise, a small smile grows behind the bars of his fingers. The careful words she'd chosen to explain what "someone" told her about Aqi and eir aspirations to stardom evaporate. "This is excellent progress. The killer is all but within my grasp, and none too soon. Abidine has deigned to let me stay to finish the investigation, but refuses to allow me to open my doors as long as we remain in the same territory."

Yokuiv sweeps the secret into a bejeweled jar and stores it in his chest of drawers. She watches him the way a mouse watches a hawk disappear past the horizon. "They won't let us perform? At all?"

"Abidine believes starving me of energy a fitting punishment for daring to seek justice for one of my own— as if *I* were the one who planned for this to happen." He barks out a derisive laugh and utters something vicious-sounding in lihilim. Leathan stiffens as he ties Renni's kerchief around her neck, then squeezes her shoulders; not hard, but enough she can feel his fingers pressing into her flesh as he guides her out the door. "But rest for tonight, Leathan. I can see the toll the investigation is taking, what it's costing you to do this."

She tries to say it's nothing; but somehow, for all the truths she's already bent, this one can't quite make it out.

Twenty-One

That didn't go the way Leathan expected, but she'd rather be surprised by Yokuiv's pleasure at her progress than the other way around. Even if she still has no idea what progress she's made, or what he'd seen in the witch's secret to make him so confident Renni's killer is as good as caught.

Indistinct music swells to drown out the twilight chirping of insects and frogs. A bassline throbs up the soles of her feet, and though she can't make out the lyrics, she recognizes the song. She'd heard it issuing out of Renni's window a hundred times at least.

She hadn't meant to head towards the party. Someone's fashioned a roughshod sound dampener around the park to keep the noise contained; Leathan suspects to keep it from aggravating their ringmaster. From high above, the lanterns Shieng and the others had enchanted cast the gyrating glow of a hundred different colors over the milling crowd. Giant paper fans waft a cool breeze overhead.

In the dark, no one notices Leathan slip along the edge of the press of bodies, reeking of sweat and sweet fragrances and cooling menthol. Troupers shout to be heard over the music, or sing along to it, jumping and swaying and laughing and crying, gulping booze for the sheer sugar-pill sweetness of it if not the true effect. It's almost like losing herself in any other crowd of strangers.

Then she sees, past the cul-de-sac of tables groaning with food and drink, beneath the crowded canopy wreathed in tiny twinkling lights, a massive screen on which cycle larger-than-life images, both moving and still, of Renni.

"Nope." Without looking at what she's grabbing, Leathan piles up a plate. Her ringmaster told her to rest, so that's what she's going to do: sequester herself in her trailer until the next time he calls for her.

A cluster of troupers chooses that moment to stumble over—a juggler, a fortune teller, and Aqi, sandwiched between eir lovers. Yokuiv's charm pulls them close, winds around them so insidiously it's like those connections have always been there. Leathan groans through her forced smile as they surround her, shuffling in so there's no escaping without elbowing them out of the way.

"How're you doing?" Aqi says. "I meant to check up on you after—"

"Great." To avoid elaborating, she slurps up a mouthful of chilled glass noodles spiced with garlic and chili. Her eyes flutter closed as she savors the bite, and the unexpected comfort of familiar flavors.

"He had good taste, didn't he?" Te'ide anchors himself on one of Aqi's arms to lean forward and shouts to be heard over the music, a syrupy pop piece from around the time Leathan joined. He hoists his own plate, piled with mountains of fried rice and sautéed greens in a thick sauce. "Renni."

When she understands, it takes her a few times to swallow past the lump in her throat. Roasted sweet potatoes, sticky steamed buns, grilled spring rolls—and so much more she wasn't able to fit, curries and pastas and casseroles, fresh fruit and salads and charred vegetables, chips and crackers and dips, confectioneries and cakes and candies. All his favorites.

Leathan jumps when Vetsla lays a cool hand on her shoulder. "I know. I still can't believe he's gone, either."

"*I* can't believe Yokuiv hasn't appointed his successor yet." The rotund fortune teller—Polinne—shifts, flakes of green glitter shimmering to the earth at their high-heeled feet, as the group's gaze swivels to them. "What? He has to know who he wants to be next, so why hasn't he said? How're we supposed to perform without a star? Assuming we ever get to perform again."

"Maybe someone should volunteer," says Aqi, ignoring the warning glare Te'ide shoots in eir direction, the way Vetsla purses her pink lips around her cocktail straw.

"Hells no." Polinne lets out a string of nervous giggles and smacks eir arm, mistaking eir soft tone for a sarcastic suggestion *they* do it. "I'm just saying, Renni's name was up in the marquee not even five minutes after Orrus struck out."

Enqirez, the juggler, slams down a plate he'd been filling with sweets. "Orrus didn't strike out. He was sabotaged."

"He wasn't." Aqi waves a hand at him. "Stop being melodramatic."

"Fuck you." A jade ring on Enqirez's middle finger flashes when he shoves the rude gesture in the trapeze artist's face. "Orrus made one tiny cut to Renni's part that Berhede didn't like, so he cut the cord."

"Why would that upset Berhede?" says Leathan, confused. "What cord? One of the wires?"

"Doesn't make it sabotage," says Aqi. "I'm no fan of Berhede's either, but—"

"It doesn't matter," interrupts Te'ide, staring hard at his lover. "Everyone knows the position's unlucky. No one survives it. Not Renni, not Orrus, not any of the others since the ceasefire."

"Not merely unlucky." Vetsla slides her arm through Te'ide's. "Cursed. The only one Yokuiv can't contain."

"It wasn't a fucking curse," Enqirez seethes, "it was *Berhede,* Renni's reaction proves it—*"*

With a beleaguered roll of their smoky cat eyes, Polinne pulls Leathan away as Enqirez and the trapeze trio continue flinging barbs. "You'd think fifteen years would be enough to let go of a grudge, but I guess there's a reason Yokuiv assigned Enqirez to the jugglers."

"Because he never drops anything?"

"Oh, I was going to say something indecent about balls. Yours is much better."

In spite of herself, Leathan snorts. "What did Berhede even *do*?"

"Depends on who you ask. Only three people know the truth, and now two of them are dead." Smiling sadly, Polinne glances over their shoulder to the canopy. "Which leaves broaching the subject with the man in question, but you'd be safer volunteering to be star."

"The position can't really be cursed."

The fortune teller takes her in over the salted rim of their drink, then shrugs. "People want something to blame for our rash of dead stars other than chance. Same reason Enqirez'd rather think his best friend was a victim of sabotage instead of circumstance. Don't tell him I said that."

Leathan holds her compact to her lips. Polinne clinks their drink against it with a laugh that jingles all the intricate beadwork on their vest. "You don't think it's Berhede's fault that Orrus struck out, then."

"No, I absolutely do," they say. "Pretty much everyone agrees on that. Even Renni—not because he found out Berhede plotted some evil scheme, whatever Enqirez claims—but because he knew Berhede could've sent out a heads-up ahead of time, and didn't, and Orrus paid the price. That's the real reason Renni ended things with him. Gods, what a spectacle. Berhede did *not* take it well."

The illusionist's tears that morning in the storage shed make a lot more sense. He wasn't crying over a man he hated, but the memory of someone he'd loved. Leathan doesn't want to linger on that thought. "Heads-up about what?"

Polinne takes another long draw from their drink before continuing. "That he was stopping his talisman trade."

Leathan nearly drops her plate of food. "Berhede traded talismans?"

"And fuck if he wasn't good at it. Too good, because it came out later a lot of troupers struggling with the ceasefire transition ended up relying almost entirely on the proceeds to make quota. Including Orrus." Polinne chomps down on a bit of mango they've dug out from their bottom of their cup. "Not that Berhede cared. He closed up shop out of the blue, no warning, no nothing, and then—"

They lift a closed fist to eye level, flinging out long-nailed fingers to mime an explosion. Leathan flinches, trying and failing not to imagine the former star's curse shattering out of his pendant.

Twenty-Two

The talismans that stalker had must have been from Berhede. There's little doubt about it in Leathan's mind—and little doubt Aqi recognized his work, yet had chosen not to say anything. She turns to ask em, but e and eir lovers are deep in the throng of troupers dancing in the middle of the park. Her few bites of food flipping and flopping in her gut, she wades in after em, keeping her head ducked to avoid anyone noticing her.

"Leathan!" E grabs her by the hands, spinning her in a gleeful half circle. Sweat slicks eir bare arms, and marks speckle eir face and neck in the shades of Vetsla and Te'ide's lipsticks. She wonders at how the three of them can swing so effortlessly from argument to affection, but maybe it's how they've managed to stay together over the decades. A sliver of jealousy stabs into her. "When's the last time you danced?"

A lifetime ago. Refusal is on her lips, but it's easier to let herself be led into the trapeze trio's circle, to let the throbbing bass move her shoulders in the tiniest of shimmies. It feels—good—to move, to not have to think, to lose herself in the music and the heat of bodies surrounding her. It almost makes her forget this isn't what she's here for.

"The talisman that stalker hexed me with," she says to Aqi when Te'ide and Vetsla are distracted. "Why didn't you tell me Berhede made it?"

Aqi's eyebrows draw together in concern. "You found out for sure?"

"Not exactly," she admits, "but who else has the skill?"

"I don't know. Renni, maybe, but I don't see why he'd give that much power to someone stalking him." E shrugs. "Still, I don't think it's good to jump to conclusions just because Berhede's an ass. I kind of get it."

"Get what?"

"Whether it was his fault or not—losing Renni must've been horrible." Eir movements grow subdued. She follows eir gaze to Te'ide and Vetsla. Longing strains eir face, though they're only an arm's length away. "Imagine going through that kind of pain."

"I try not to."

Aqi lets out a hollow laugh. "All I'm saying is—I can relate."

"Is that why you want to be star?"

E grimaces, angling eir back to eir lovers so they won't be able to hear. "Trust me, I don't. It was a—desperate idea I had, because my retirement's coming up so soon."

"I always thought you'd joined together."

"Nope," e says. "There are a couple dozen years between me and Vetsla, and half as much between her and Te'ide. So yeah, I considered volunteering. Deluded myself into thinking all the extra magic I'd earn would help me find a way for us all to break out together, because if we don't, chances are, once I'm gone, I'll never see either of them again."

Leathan's chest constricts. "Almost makes you wish you'd never fallen for them in the first place."

"What? No, of course not." The trapeze artists stares at her in horror. "No matter what happens, I'll never regret being with them. Anyone who's ever loved anyone would tell you the same—even Berhede."

Somehow she doubts that.

Maneuvering around the party is like steering through an ocean pockmarked with whirlpools, all trying to drag Leathan into cloistered cliques of circusfolk if she lists close enough for Yokuiv's charm to snare anyone. She learns, if ever a stray hand lands on her elbow or someone looks set to intercept her chosen path, how to save herself getting sucked under, how to hook her gaze on something else in the distance and heave herself away with a smile and a placating *sorry, I'll be right back,* without ever slowing.

But gods, is it exhausting.

She's on the verge of leaving when she spots Berhede, hunched alone against one of the canopy's metal posts, yellow-flecked eyes flat and dry and fixed on the images of Renni on the screen. He's changed out of his clothes from last night into a rumpled navy shirt belted into faded khakis. At least three bodies' worth of empty space separates him and the nearest troupers. Mostly they ignore him, though every so often someone shifts and glances back with a mixture of curiosity and uncertainty. They must be wondering the same thing as Leathan: why is he *here*, of all places?

Except she's also wondering other things. Like if he's kept up his talisman trade in secret. If he's the wandering artisan the mystic meant, or the one who'd provided the stalker her cache.

If Orrus might not be the only star whose blood is on his hands.

As Leathan picks her way towards him across the edge of the crowd, making sure to keep the screen behind her, she watches him watch Renni. The light from the projector plays in fluid shadows across his angular features, his expression slack and impenetrable beneath his gold-dusted beard. The fortune teller's warning rings in her ears, harmonizing with her own misgivings she'll be able to coax him to speak to her about things he's confided in no one else, even with Yokuiv's power smoothing the way.

She makes sure to let him see her coming, and restrains the urge to fight it as her ringmaster's charm wraps around him, nice and snug.

"Some party," she says. "Do they—is it always like this? When someone …"

"Dunno." He picks at what's left of the label on his sweating bottle of beer with nails bitten to the quick. "I don't usually go."

"So why'd you come tonight?"

His eyes flit down to her neck, to the kerchief tied at her throat. Her fingers worry the fabric. Can he tell it's Renni's work? "Same reason as you."

"Berhede." She leans in conspiratorially. "The food's always free."

The illusionist stares at her for one long second until laughter erupts out of him, straight from his belly. A couple of troupers bounce concerned gazes from Leathan to Berhede and back. She gestures a quick reassurance and grins to reinforce it. Berhede doesn't seem to notice; if he does, he doesn't seem to care.

"Fuck." He scrapes a hand through his mane of dark curls. "I wish I could do that."

"Do what?"

"Pretend the bastard meant nothing to me." Before she can argue, his gaze drifts behind her. "There you are again."

Thrown off balance by the abruptness of the odd statement, Leathan follows Berhede's gaze to the giant screen, and sees herself, standing outside the big top backstage door with Renni. He's in an old costume—celestial and stunning in a nebula of jewel-tone layers of taffeta and glitter and feathers—holding her arms out by the wrists, grinning his crooked tooth grin as he takes her in. He's saying something she can't hear over the chatter of the crowd.

Leathan has no memory of this specific moment, but she remembers her costume, hundreds of tiny rhinestones swirling around her torso and limbs, layers of slick gray sateen torrenting off her shoulders and hips, hair twisted up in a crash of lightning bolts and blue gems strung across her brow. It was her first one, which means this image was captured right after she'd joined the Extravaganza. Perhaps even the night of her debut. What a blur of nauseated terror that had been—though she doesn't look scared, as Renni twirls her in circles to make the satin swirl. She's hunched in embarrassment, but there's a faint, pleased twist at the corners of her mouth.

The image changes. She keeps staring even though she doesn't want to, because Berhede was right—there she is again, training in her nook at the gym while Renni balances in a one-handed stand on a mat nearby. And again, standing in line at the canteen for dinner, while behind her he gestures in telling a story. And again, leaping across the stage during a show from a couple runs ago, while from off-stage Renni watches with pride in his bright brown eyes. And again, and again. Never prominent—Renni's the focus, of course—and hardly the only other trouper, but more often than not, more often than she expects, she's somewhere in the frame.

"Don't cry," mutters Berhede. "Asshole's not worth it."

She jerks out of her stupor, swipes away the fat tears dripping off her chin. The illusionist's eyes are puffy, cheeks and nose ruddy. She sees him again as he was in the shed. Sees the silk heart she'd picked up from the floor, and takes a stab at it. "You seemed to think so this morning, or you wouldn't have left that talisman at his jewel box."

"Yeah, well. That was this morning." He takes a sullen swig of beer. "Before I found out he was leaving."

"What?" She reels as the rest of the conversation she'd planned in her head gets yanked out from under her. "I thought he was still years away from ... retiring ..."

She trails off as the realization washes over her, slow and suffocating. There are only three ways out of a contract— well, four, including "their soul disincorporating from their physical form": striking out, reaching the end of the hundred-year term, or—

"Huh. I thought he would've told you." He goes to take another pull from his beer, realizes it's empty, and lets out an incredulous scoff into its neck. "Sorry. I know it's callous, but it's kind of a relief someone else finally knows what it feels like when Renni fucks them over. If it's any consolation, at least he didn't turn the entire outfit against you."

She realizes she's gripping the kerchief at her throat again, forces her fingers to hang loose at her sides. "You're not making any sense."

"I thought something was up last night when he put on that fucking song—" Berhede's voice cracks, and his throat bobs up and down for a few seconds as he tries to swallow. Then he shakes his head, lobs the empty bottle into a trash can, and pushes towards the drinks table for a refill. Leathan, at a loss for what else to do, follows. "Joke's on me for thinking it meant anything but one final parting shot, but I get the last laugh, because someone went and murdered the bastard right after he broke his curse."

"If he'd found a way to break out, he'd have said," Leathan insists. "He'd have helped the rest of us figure it out—he wouldn't have—"

"Abandoned you?" Berhede throws the words like a punch. "His pendant was gone. Not missing—gone. That's why your trace couldn't find it. Because he destroyed it when he broke his curse. Face it, Leathan. He never gave a fuck about anyone but himself."

Of all the things she could say to refute his logic, what leaves her lips is a hissed: "I don't believe you."

His face shutters. The connection Yokuiv's charm has built between them twangs like a string about to snap. "No one ever does."

TWENTY-THREE

Berhede snatches another beer and storms off into the night. With a feral growl, Leathan pours every alcoholic liquid she can reach into a cup. It'll taste like shit, but she doesn't care—she wants it to pack a punch strong enough to numb her, at least for the few seconds it takes for her contractual protections to cleanse the substance from her system.

The illusionist was jumping to conclusions, or flat out lying to cover his ass. She doesn't believe Renni would've found a way to break his curse and kept it to himself, or left without a word to her—to anyone; that someone with the luxury of parting on his own terms would choose to skip the goodbyes.

Would choose to say goodbye in the first place.

Before-her pipes up then. It's only ever been sensations, or instincts; vague, fleeting, unnameable things easy to ignore. This time, though, Leathan all but hears her saying,

Hypocrite; saying, *You were prepared to do the exact same thing yesterday.*

That's different. She has no one to say goodbye to.

That's not true and you know it.

A hand rests on her forearm as she grabs for a half-empty bottle of dark rum. She startles; she hadn't even felt Yokuiv's charm through her haze of desperation to get smashed.

"That won't work the way you think," Casallie signs, silver charm bracelet glinting in the lantern light. "Protections'll kick into overdrive to compensate, and you won't get so much as a tingle. Do yourself a favor and dump that into the dirt."

Leathan's tempted to ignore her advice and drink it anyway, but then the fans tilt their way and she gets a whiff of what she's made, and the stench makes her stomach try to kick itself out of her. Gagging, she upends it over the weedy grass behind the table. "Worth a shot."

"Trust me, I know. But I have a better way."

The contortionist splashes rum into a clean cup, then surreptitiously tips one of the rainbow crystals of her bracelet over the rim. A single droplet of glittering, opalescent liquid pearls out of the crystal and tumbles into the rum with a hiss.

Leathan lifts the cup to her face, jerking away when astringent magic burns her nose. Something about the weave is familiar, and not because it's almost as rancid as the concoction she'd dumped. "What is this?"

"Something I came up with after a couple decades of Extravaganza life got to be a bit—much." Her brown eyes go distant as she reattaches the crystal, but she shakes her head to dispel whatever passing memories clouded her thoughts. "Now the alcohol can affect you like when you were mortal, at least until the morning."

The only reason Leathan doesn't drop the cup is because her entire body goes rigid. She knows why she recognizes the weave. "This bypasses our protections?"

"*Shh.*" The contortionist shoves down Leathan's flailing hand. "Not everyone knows about this, and for good reason. I'd be screwed if it ever got back to Yokuiv I figured out a loophole."

"Is this the bracelet you told me about? The one you thought Renni stole?" Red blossoms in the contortionist's sandy cheeks, and her eyes dart away. That's a yes. Leathan grabs her shoulders to make Casallie look at her again. "You never did say where you found it."

"I didn't find it." The contortionist shakes her head. "When I got back to my trailer, after Yokuiv finished questioning me, it was on top of my bookshelf—but that's not where I keep it. Someone else put it there."

"Were all the crystals still attached?"

Tears overflow in Casallie's eyes. Her hands shake so violently Leathan can hardly follow, but she already knows the answer. "One was gone."

"If one drop lets you get drunk, then what does an entire fucking crystal-full do?" Leathan doesn't mean to sign so harshly. Casallie flinches away.

"I don't know—I don't know, I never give anyone more than that." She twists the bracelet around her wrist in quick, sporadic loops. "I only make this so we can get a little respite. Especially on nights like tonight."

"Who knows about this? Your—loophole? Where you keep it?"

Her eyes beg Leathan to understand, beseech forgiveness. "I know what you're thinking, because I've spent the last twenty-four hours wondering the same thing. Wondering which of my friends took it, used it to k-kill another of my friends—and I know I should've told Yokuiv, but I'm terrified what he'll do to me if he finds out I have a workaround. Gods, I should've listened to Renni, he was always on me to get rid of it, and if I had maybe then he wouldn't be—"

"Casallie." Leathan presses as much urgency into her signs as she can. "Who knows?"

"Only people I trust. Or thought I did." The contortionist gives a hiccuping laugh. "N'verly, Shieng and her crew, Polinne—you, of course—"

Without thinking, Leathan takes a long, steadying sip of her drink, realizing her mistake the instant the liquid hits her tongue, warm and smooth and smoky from the rum, bitter and warped from the loophole. She freezes, holding the liquid in her mouth as the contortionist lists off a quarter of the outfit. She should spit it out into the cup—this is the thing that killed Renni, or rather paved the way for his death—but her chest still aches, and she's so desperate to make it go away, and a single drop won't get rid of the entirety of her protections, and she has a long night ahead of her yet.

So she swallows.

The loophole creeps up on her like a sunrise as, one by one, she seeks out each trouper Casallie named who has or had facial hair. Yokuiv's charm makes them all greet her with wide smiles and warmth, and even though she suspects them of murder, she can't help feeling a pang of— something; guilt, regret?—for the fake friendships she's cultivating. When Renni's killer is caught and the charm breaks, what will happen to these connections? Will they vanish without a trace? Or will it hurt, like her curse, and leave scars?

Somehow either outcome seems equally horrific.

She tries not to think about what that means, to focus on the task at hand, but she forgets what that is. She looks, but all she has in her hand is another cup of liquor she can't remember pouring. How many of these has she had? The sea of strangers who aren't quite strangers anymore swirls around her, and she no longer has the fortitude or the wherewithal, or the will, to avoid the undertow of every trouper Yokuiv's charm tangles around.

"Remember that one time," someone says about Renni, and Leathan does.

"Remember that one time," she hears herself say back, instead of cleverly asking about bracelets or tea or talismans or missing pendants; and they do.

On, and on, wave after wave, until she could drown in memories of him, of them—of all of them, together. Yet she doesn't. Every time it happens, she feels buoyed. Lifted. Like she feels during a show, brimming with mortal energy, swept up in the flow of the performance; except there's no stage, no audience, no choreography or costumes.

It's so much better this way, whispers before-her. Leathan worries at the enchantment like a loose tooth, shuddering at the spikes of pain radiating out with each stubborn, useless prod. *Isn't it?*

The next morning she remembers none of it, which—with her protections taking care of the hangover that would otherwise have left her curled in the fetal position praying for sweet release—is the only way she knows she had a good night.

That, and she wakes up in someone else's trailer.

TWENTY-FOUR

It's the smell of the pillow beneath her squished cheek that tips Leathan off. She braces to extract herself from the sleep-heavy embrace of a lover or lovers, but there's no one else in the bunk with her. With a groggy sigh she relaxes back into her repose, inhaling velvety florals and warm herbals, subtle peppermint, nutty shea.

She sits bolt upright. Takes in the cosmetics cluttering the vanity, the pile of clothes spilling out of the closet, the shelves crammed with albums and tea.

At least there's no severed arm on the carpet.

Leathan buries her face in her hands and laughs, then sobs. Quiet, heaving sobs, like her entire soul is squeezing out through her eyes, dribbling out of her nose. She gasps for breath, grabs at her throat, fingers seeking the comfort of the kerchief.

It's gone.

For a few panicked moments Leathan can't find her compact, either; but it's shoved under one of the many pillows and cushions piled on Renni's bunk. In her haste she casts the trace too wide, across the entirety of the trailer and not just her neck. She hisses at her clumsiness, but it's too late to fix the weave; the spell shimmers and settles over the grooves of what should be there, but isn't. Faint outlines of Renni's compact and record player appear; but also some clothes, an album or two, some cannisters of tea, and the lumpy shape of an over-shoulder bag.

She sinks back onto the bunk. Stars aren't allowed out of circus bounds at all, yet Renni had packed a bag to leave.

Berhede was right.

A scream builds in her throat. As she grabs one of Renni's ridiculous pillows to stifle it, she notices the trace's impression of a pair of keychains on his bookshelf, the same size and shape as the melty glitter cats she'd given him.

She stares. She must be imagining things. She wasn't important enough to tell her he was breaking out, so why would he have taken those keychains with him?

Not that it matters, now that he's dead.

Wait.

She rakes her hands through the bed-headed mess of her hair. Renni'd been killed before he could leave, which means his bag and all the things he'd stuffed into it should still be here.

Had the killer had taken it? Or the stalker, and Leathan hadn't noticed because she'd been so distracted by the record player and their dead star's voice crooning in her ear? Something else to tell Yokuiv in addition to what she'd learned at the party last night—which was, what? Trying to remember, she grabs an ornate turquoise hand mirror from Renni's vanity and angles it at the glittering trace of blue and brass fabric around her neck. It's nearly solid; it must not be far.

The construct guarding Renni's door swivels a single opal eye to regard her as she emerges. She gets vague flashes of leaning against its marble torso and pleading, cajoling, to be let in, saying it owed her a favor for her help with the mortal, saying it was all part of the investigation. Before she can decide if she should apologize or say thank you, the construct looks away with a soft scraping of stone against stone. She settles for a perfunctory pat on its arm.

She follows the trace all the way to the fairgrounds. She doesn't remember leaving the backyard last night, but then again, she doesn't remember most of what happened after imbibing the loophole. Its brightening outline leads her through the silent stalls to the shrouded entrance of the Tent of Illusions.

Of course her kerchief ended up in Berhede's show.

"Hello?" No answer. Unsurprising; it's too early for Berhede to be here on a normal day, and there's no use prepping when the Extravaganza's been put on indefinite hiatus.

Stepping into another trouper's show feels as boundary-crossing as going into their trailer, especially when they're absent—and especially when they're someone she last parted with on not the greatest of terms, and also suspects of being a murderer.

She drops the hand mirror; no need for it here, where looking glasses of all shapes and sizes catch her reflection, throwing it back a hundredfold. The trace around her neck is the only source of light in the entire tent. The reflections give her the sensation of bobbing through a galaxy of stars.

At a polished wooden dais in the center, Leathan notices an angular shape behind a towering mirror. The trace is so bright, she has to squint as she kneels behind the mirror, at the foot of a large wooden trunk where Berhede must store all his props for the show, and where her kerchief must be.

It's locked, of course, with a padlock enchanted for security. A bit excessive for cheap props. She picks the complicated knots of the weave apart, just loose enough so she can pry open the lid to fit her hand through. It's an awkward affair, tilting her head so the light of the trace can illuminate the trunk's contents at an angle that still allows her to peer inside. She glimpses a flash of brass and blue; her fingers brush soft fabric, and the familiar charm brushes back, though there's a sense of urgency to its touch, like it's trying to shove her away.

"Come on so we can get the fuck out of here," she mutters. She gives up her line of sight, wedging herself closer to reach further into the trunk. At last she manages to nab the kerchief, but when she tries to pull it out, it jerks in her hand. It's caught on something.

After several frustrating seconds, it finally comes free, so suddenly the force of her pull sends her tumbling back on her ass. The trace vanishes, plunging her into darkness. Something heavy and rubbery and dripping with putrid magic lands in her lap. Unease fluttering in her gut, Leathan conjures a tiny floating orb of pale blue light.

It's an arm.

Leathan shoves it off her with a scream, scrambling back on all fours. It lands with a dull thud at the foot of the trunk.

"Fuck," she hisses, and forces herself to crawl closer so she can get a better look. It's severed at the shoulder, hand clutched tight around the kerchief, blood stinking of corrupted magic. There's no tattoo; the skin and hair is a shade lighter; and it's a right arm, not a left. Not Renni's—someone else's. "Fuck, fuck, fuck."

On the waxy forefinger glints a jade ring. A jade ring she'd last seen Enqirez flipping in Aqi's face. No—she'd seen it after that. A flash of jade through lantern light. A fist landing on a gold-dusted beard. Yelling, jeering, someone diving in to pull two brawling bodies apart.

Rapid footfalls break her concentration. Yokuiv's charm twitches, and she whirls. Berhede stands in the middle of the dais, chest heaving. Specks of gold still glitter in his beard.

"I heard you scream, are you—" His gaze flits from her stricken face to Enqirez's arm. The purple duffel bag he clutches thuds to the wooden floor. "The fuck?"

She rises slowly, cracking open her compact behind her. "Did Enqirez pick a fight with you last night because he found out?"

"Find out what?"

"That another star was dead because of you."

It hits him like a blow. He takes half a step back, shaking his head. "You can't think I would've—you know me—"

"I know you hated Renni for leaving you," she snaps. "For making everyone think Orrus striking out was your fault."

"That's not true—"

"Fifteen years he made your life miserable. Then you found out he was going to break his curse. It wasn't fair, that he'd get to be free, and you'd have to stay here suffering."

"Leathan," he begs, voice cracking. "I would never hurt him. Never, no matter how much he hurt me."

"You already had one star's blood on your hands—what was one more?"

"I didn't kill him!"

"No." The connection between them strains. She thinks of the two strikes about to be cleared from her contract, her debt to Renni paid—and tears it out. "You just dosed his tea, then gave his mortal stalker the talismans to do it for you."

Berhede's swollen eyes narrow. He grabs the compact clipped to his belt, but before he can weave anything, a construct materializes behind him, half a dozen limbs snapping around him like marble chains. A sandal flies off as he kicks his feet, bellowing in his vain struggle for freedom. The construct clamps a stone hand down on his mouth to silence him as Yokuiv steps up onto the dais.

"I told you to rest." Her ringmaster's scolding is tempered by a triumphant smile tugging at his lips, the gentle hand he rests on her shoulder. "Instead you've caught me a killer."

Yokuiv's charm unravels around her, and in the same moment she kens the two struck seals on her contract have been made whole again. It should feel like a release of shackles, like stepping back from the edge—like relief—but it doesn't. She only feels emptied. Hollowed out.

The construct wrests Berhede from the Tent of Illusions. Outside a crowd has gathered, and there are sobs and shouts and jeers. The illusionist shrinks back against his captor, nostrils flaring, eyes rolling wildly. Leathan looks away before they can land on her. She can't bring herself to meet his gaze, to see the betrayal there.

Or rather the lack of it, now he's no longer charmed into thinking they're friends.

She doesn't know which would be worse.

"I know you are angry and hurt." Yokuiv's soft voice projects to the far corners of the Extravaganza. "I know you want justice for Renni, and now poor Enqirez—and that you shall have—" He pauses to indulge a chorus of vicious cheers. "—after we make our preparations to go."

Reluctantly the gathered troupers disperse to get ready to relocate, glaring after Berhede's struggling form until the construct drags him out of sight. A few curious stares land on Leathan, but with magic no longer drawing them to her, no one looks at her for long. All the connections the charm helped form between them over the last day and a half wither like dead leaves. She turns to the big top without a backwards glance and tries to tell herself they were never real to begin with.

TWENTY-FIVE

Two hundred troupers packing crates magicked against the compression of squeezing the outfit through space and time to the next territory should give the circus an air of activity, but to Leathan, floating from one rote task to another, it feels stagnant. Then again, that could be the humidity, which grows more oppressive as the morning crawls into afternoon.

As the big top comes down, Leathan catches a whiff of golden hour sun. She fights back an alarmed scowl at the faint honeysuckle scent, the downy softness settling around her like an arm flung over her shoulders, nudging her *this way*.

Why the hells is Zuna here? Yokuiv informed Phenomenae he caught Renni's killer, that the Extravaganza is relocating. There's nothing more for them to spy on.

Before-her stirs, groggy and hopeful. Have they come to say goodbye?

Or to play another game?

Whatever the reason, Leathan won't answer their summons. Not again.

But the magic follows her as she weaves through the deflated body of the big top to collect support struts. It tugs on the hem of her shirt, the lace of her shoe, a flyaway strand of her hair, anything it can reach. Before-her is no help, leaning towards it every time. Unable to ignore it anymore, Leathan shoos the summons away with a hiss. A handful of nearby performers winding wires pause in their tearful reminiscing about Enqirez to look at her in concern.

"Mosquitoes," she says meekly, fleeing to stash her bundle of struts in its crate. Zuna's relentless hounding and before-her's urging are going to get either or both of them in trouble if she doesn't do something. She glances over her shoulder at the others to make sure their attention's moved on, then follows the trail of Phenomenae power.

When she reaches the edge of the outfit, the summons cuts off like lights dousing after a show. She gropes for the last whiff, even as she hopes Zuna's given up and left. Then she rounds a corner and catches the profile of their mask under an awning a few meters beyond the threshold. Leathan crouches behind a stack of crates, inching forward until she's pressed up against the border between mortal reality and the Extravaganza.

The spy isn't alone. A large bearded figure corners them against the brick wall of a laundry mat. For a second Leathan thinks it's Berhede, that somehow he's escaped, until the figure shifts. Leathan recognizes her angry features from the Phenomenae advertisements; the fire dancer with flames erupting out of her skull and jaw, except now it's not flames, but thick, curly brown hair glimmering red in the sun.

They're arguing, too quietly to hear. Leathan weaves one end of an amplifying charm around one of her earrings and anchors the other to a pebble before skipping it across the asphalt towards the two Phenomenae troupers. This close to the Extravaganza, they shouldn't notice the spell among its ambient power; it's a single drop of rain in a downpour.

"—can't make contact until he's safe," Zuna's saying when Leathan's talisman skitters to a stop shy of their heel. "She could help—"

"She fucked us in the first place." The fire dancer's baritone rumbles like thunder. "And you're fucking us more, risking everything for some ridiculous—"

Leathan misses the final word when Zuna shoves the fire dancer, hard. Even without magic behind the blow, the fire dancer stumbles backwards; with a growl, she shoves Zuna right back. The spy stumbles onto their ass. Something crunches—their tail bone, their wrist? Leathan winces in spite of herself.

"Feel better?"

"No," Zuna seethes. "Let me try again."

The fire dancer sighs. Then her eyes narrow at the pavement. "The fuck is that?"

Leathan ducks out of sight, ear full of garbled voices; there comes a crunch, and the magic snuffs out. She peeks a hair's breadth around the crates. Zuna steps towards the Extravaganza, an eager-eyed expression on their mask, but their companion grabs them by their upper arm with a shake of her head, tugging them down the alley.

For a second Zuna looks like they're considering fighting back, but they relent. Leathan sags against her hiding spot, watching them go, watching them look over their shoulder as if expecting her to dash out after them. Before-her urges her to do just that; she sandwiches her head between her hands to squash the thought, and catches a glimmer of something on the ground where the fire dancer knocked Zuna onto their ass. As soon as the Phenomenae troupers are out of sight, she casts out a thread of magic like a fishing line.

The spell deposits into her waiting palms, cracked into three distinct pieces, one of the kitty keychains she gave Renni.

The pieces tumble from her numbed hands. She staggers away from them like they're a timed jinx about to detonate.

The crunch she heard when Zuna fell wasn't their bones, but the keychain shattering. They had it in their pocket.

They'd been in Renni's trailer.

Reality lurches out from under her. She'd helped Yokuiv catch the wrong killer. It had been Phenomenae after all.

Zuna learned the outfit's routines, their habits, so they could kill Renni and frame his death to make even Yokuiv believe it had been one of his. They knew they had the perfect scapegoat in Berhede since the entire outfit hated him already. Knew Renni loved tea, knew about his stalker, about Casallie's loophole; even went so far as to leverage the fire dancer's resemblance to Berhede. Killed Enqirez and planted his arm in the illusionist's trunk as the final nail in the illusionist's coffin—

She should've known better than to trust Zuna. They'd led her around by the nose all yesterday, making her forget they were anything but her enemy.

Agony lances through her heart, agony like she hasn't felt since the last time her curse took her. This isn't right—

whatever connection had grown between her and them, it isn't *real*, isn't supposed to be able to *hurt*—

Gasping for breath, she snatches up the broken keychain. She should tell Yokuiv, but he might not believe her without proof. She needs to get that first, and fast. There's less than an hour until the outfit relocates.

The VIP ticket to Phenomenae is still crumpled under her curse pendant. She stuffs it into the breast pocket of her denim jacket, slips her pendant under her shirt. She wishes she had thought to reclaim the kerchief from Enqirez's hand, wishes she had the blue and brass fabric to tie around her neck. It should be with her, when she performs one last time for Zuna.

Twenty-Six

Phenomenae is minuscule. No arch, no fairground stalls or side attractions; just a single silver- and blue-striped tent and a haphazard scattering of trailers.

The lights are on in the largest, unintelligible voices spilling out of a propped open window. Leathan hallucinates Renni's among them, and has to fight not to tear the ticket into a million tiny pieces as she pulls it from her pocket. It tingles under her touch, anticipatory. She forces herself to walk slow, hands off her compact; she doesn't want the spy suspecting anything until it's too late. She has to make it look like she's not sure. Like she doesn't know what she's doing. Like she's scared.

It helps all of those things are true.

She hesitates at the edge of their threshold, the bend in reality where Phenomenae shouldn't be, but is. She holds her breath, and crosses inside.

Zuna appears in two heartbeats. Stare at her for another two, unmoving.

"You came." Their voice sounds clogged, like they've been crying. Leathan wants to slap the mask off them. "You're here."

"You left before I could come find you." The truth. Tell the truth, right until it twists into a lie.

"I had to," they whisper. "I'm sorry."

Not yet. But they will be.

They reach towards her. "Leathan—"

"Come have a drink with me before we relocate?" She steps out of reach, lips curled into an enticing half-grin, taking pleasure in the way they shudder. "Promise I won't spill it on you this time."

They glance to the trailers. "I can't."

Her grin flickers, fades. She drops her head, pretending to hide her disappointment, though of course she makes sure they catch a glimpse. "I understand."

They close the distance between them. She lets them touch her, feel her shaking. Fuck, she hates how much she—how much *before-her*—wants to lean into their arms. She does. Just a little. To heighten the performance. Zuna makes a strangled noise, their fingers tightening around her. They pull her towards the trailers. "Come inside. With us. Now that you're here I can show you—"

She forces herself away, shakes her head. She's not going any further into their outfit than she has to, or entertaining any more of their lies. "I should go."

"Wait." Zuna's fingers scrape for hers, but she retreats out of Phenomenae bounds before they can grab her again. She hunches over and hurries down the street. She hates having her back to the enemy, but she has to, or the lure won't work.

Ten seconds pass. Twenty. She thinks it hasn't worked anyway, but then the shadows in front of her shimmer and fold. Phenomenae magic glides over her skin, and Zuna's there, chest heaving, their gold and glass curse pendant gleaming on their breast. She catches a glimpse of bronze inside. "I can't let you go back to the Extravaganza."

"You don't have a choice," Leathan says, and springs the trap around them.

The barrier she'd prepared carves them out of the human world. The spy is stuck inside these scant few meters of street with her until she dies, or they do. Preferably neither; she wants to bring them back to her ringmaster alive. Watch him wring the truth from their lying mouth.

The paint on Zuna's mask swirls in shock as Leathan transforms into her costume. She doesn't even care it leaves her pendant visible. "What are you doing?"

"You don't get to act betrayed." She throws the shattered keychain to the pavement at their feet.

They take a startled step back, shoulders tense, and spread their hands towards her in a supplicating gesture. "If you'd let me explain—"

Leathan flings out a hex, barbed and ugly and sharp. They deflect it, but it glances across their pendant with a screech of glass. With a pained grunt, Zuna lunges to the side, slipping into the shadows.

"I don't want to fight you."

"Coward," she spits. She can still sense them. They may not have meant to, but they spent the last two months teaching her how to find them in dark places, how to see them even when they're hiding. She lashes out at corners, at movements in her peripherals. She hates that she can feel them like this, like they're part of her.

"Please, Leathan," they whisper in her ear. "He wouldn't want this."

She screams, flinging magic out in tangled, angry bursts, feeling a swell of righteous retribution every time something hits the spy and they grunt in pain. The asphalt explodes; the streetlamps bend and break; the walls crumble around them. Her pendant is cold against her chest.

Quick and slippery, Zuna darts through the shadows, until Leathan fools them with a feint and lassos magic around their ankles. They skid along what's left of the pavement and struggle to right themself, writhing against the spell as it slithers up their prone form. She makes it squeeze, makes the rope grow thorns that dig into their flesh. Their contractual protections push back against the magic, healing as fast as the spell can pierce them.

Phenomenae power shatters through her barrier. Leathan is flung backwards, her compact torn from her belly. Her costume disintegrates as she crashes into a half-demolished wall. Every bone in her back breaks. Blood sprays out over her chin as ribs pierce her lungs. For a second she's suffocating, and then her protections take over and stitch her back together.

A tall woman in deep golden silks cuts Zuna free with one sharp-nailed hand, using the other to press gentle magic around Leathan's limbs, flattening her to the ground. Phenomenae's ringmaster, even more beautiful and terrible than the posters.

"Shh," soothes Abidine. Leathan hacks up pieces of lung and tissue, struggling for her compact as she feels all her rage and fight seep away, like the power holding her to the earth is leeching it out of her. Hands cup her jaw. Woozily she stares into the woman's face. Her dark brown cheeks are freckled with pockmarks, her eyes black holes that suck Leathan in, her hair in small bejeweled braids twisted in intricate knots at her temples. Leathan could stare at her for the rest of her life, which probably isn't much longer. "Sleep."

Leathan musters all her strength to fight the command. It's a losing battle. Abidine isn't as powerful as Yokuiv, but she's still lihilim. She doesn't bother to watch the enchantment drag Leathan under, but addresses her spy. The magic muddies Leathan's ears too much to make out what they're saying.

As she feels her consciousness slip away, her hand brushes her compact; she dips one clumsy, heavy finger into the diminished well of magic within. A burnished beetle manifests in her slackening palm, skitters down the ravaged street, and disappears down a drainage gate. Leathan watches it go with fading vision, hoping her call for help gets to Yokuiv in time.

TWENTY-SEVEN

Leathan wakes upside down, squinting into bright light, wrists and ankles clamped by metal rings to a smooth, hard surface. A burning ball slams next to her head. She recoils, gagging on the chemical smell of singed paint and wood.

"Oh, good." Leathan recognizes the voice of the bearded fire dancer. "You're up."

"Don't be a dick, Mabeqir," Zuna snaps.

"Like she wasn't a dick when she jumped you?" Five more balls of flame appear, hazy points of orange-red. "She shouldn't even be here. Thinking you could sway her with that keychain is one thing, but giving her a fucking *VIP* ticket?"

"I told you, he had her investigating, and we needed her on our side—"

"You mean *you* needed her—"

"There's no purpose bickering about what's already done." The Phenomenae ringmaster's large shadow falls over Leathan, and she flinches; but Abidine only rotates the wheel Leathan's pinioned to until she's upright. "We might as well see what use we can make of her."

Leathan's watering eyes dart around. They've brought her inside Phenomenae's big top. Behind Mabeqir and Zuna hover the aerialists she'd seen on the outfit's posters, and someone else. A recent recruit?

Abidine beckons them forward. Leathan tenses. The figure comes into view, right hand twisting into the hem of his mesh shirt, left sleeve knotted beneath the stump of his shoulder. There's only the barest hint of make-up on his face, but Leathan would recognize that crooked tooth grin anywhere, even if his lips are quivering so much he can't hold it in place.

"Hi, Leathan," says Renni.

"No," is all she can say, because it can't be him. She saw the bloody mess of his trailer, kenned the poison in his tea. It's a trick. An illusion.

"This isn't how I wanted you to find out," the fake Renni says, and fuck if it doesn't sound exactly like him. "I was going to tell everyone, once it was safe, once it was all over, but—things didn't go exactly the way we planned."

"No thanks to a certain someone," mutters Mabeqir.

"Hush," chides Abidine as Zuna sputters a response, though she sounds amused. "Let the man tell his story."

The fake chews the left side of his cheek, the way the real Renni did whenever he felt guilty. "I don't even know how to start."

"Then don't," Leathan snaps, surprising herself and the Phenomenae troupe both. "I don't want to hear it, whatever story you've come up with to try and—I don't know what. Recruit me? Get me to turn on my outfit? If you think I'd do anything to let any more of them come to harm—if you think I'd join you after you murdered my best friend—"

"What?" Not-Renni crosses the ring in two long strides to stand in front of her, blocking the others from view. "Say that again."

"My best friend." Leathan bites off the words like they're barbed wire, choking on tears and the soft peppermint and flower scent of him.

"You fucking brat," he crows. "Took you long enough to admit it."

Suddenly he's crying too, big fat tears that make his dark cheeks shine like the night sky reflected in the ocean, and Leathan is forced to accept that no magic, lihilim or otherwise, could render so lifelike a copy of a person right down to his smell; down to such minute expressiveness, like the way he calls her "brat" like it's a term of endearment;

the utter tenderness with which he frees her from the cuffs and catches her in his arm as she falls from the wheel. Distantly, she's aware of Abidine ushering the others from the tent, of the soft susurration of a curtain swishing shut across the entrance, of voices arguing in low, harsh whispers outside.

"It's really you," she keeps saying, delirious with joy and disbelief and anger and confusion and too many other things to name. If she were still mortal she'd look like an exploding nebula. "How—"

Then she notices there's no gold chain around his neck, no thimble-sized glass bauble beneath the loose knit of his shirt. She jerks away.

His arm lilts in the air after her as she takes another half step back. "What?"

"You broke out," she says. "You broke out, and you were so desperate that no one else know, you had Phenomenae help fake your own death rather than tell us— tell me—"

"That's not true," he says sharply. "I mean, the part about being desperate and faking my death is, but I didn't break my curse. If I'd figured that out, I'd have hollered it from the big top so loud everyone in the Extravaganza— hells, everyone in the entire Circuit would've heard."

"You're not wearing your pendant."

He chews on his cheek again. "I don't need to in here."

In here. Inside Phenomenae, he means, which makes no sense until it does. Troupers don't need to wear their pendant inside their own outfit.

He must see the betrayal curdling her features because he cuts her off before she opens her mouth. "I know I'm telling it all wrong, but I've had to keep this secret for fifteen years or risk people getting killed—worse than killed—"

Fifteen years. "Does this have to do with what happened to Orrus? What Berhede did to him?"

"It wasn't Berhede," Renni spits in a sharp, violently protective tone she's never heard him use. His nostrils flare. "It was Yokuiv. I saw it happen—saw him peel Orrus open and suck out his soul—power-hungry bastard, I'd always wondered how he'd sustained his strength in peacetime, and now I had my answer. But he saw me standing there, and I couldn't move, I was so scared—next thing I knew we were in his office, and he told me I was star now, the next fruit he was ripening on the vine, and said if I ever tried to escape the Extravaganza or tell anyone what I'd seen, he'd make—" His voice cracks, and he swallows before continuing. "—he'd make Berhede suffer, and make me watch."

At some point Leathan has covered her mouth with her hands, trying keep the horror inside her from spilling out in a scream. "You did this to protect him. You still love him."

"I tried to make it look like he and I were done, at first. Hoped Yokuiv wouldn't target him if he thought it didn't give him leverage over me, but of course he didn't fucking buy it. Only thing leaving Berhede did was make him hate me, and make the rest of the outfit hate him, and I couldn't even tell them not to without risking his life." Renni lets out a hiccoughed laugh and paces half circles in the dirt. "I wish I could say I planned my great escape then and there, but I didn't. I spiraled for a few years, thinking I couldn't do shit but wait until my soul was ripe enough for Yokuiv's picking, and served me right for hurting the man I loved more than anything out of some misguided attempt to save him. Then a liaison from Phenomenae contacted me, part of some last-ditch effort Abidine was making to save her outfit by poaching troupers. I turned her down at first, still too scared for Berhede—but at the party at the end of that run I realized, if Phenomenae was willing to take the risk, there was a way out."

"A loophole," whispers Leathan. "You *did* steal Casallie's bracelet the other night."

"Just the one crystal," he says, abashed. "I'd have taken less, but I wasn't sure how much I actually needed to disincorporate my soul."

Her jaw drops, actually drops. "If you misjudged, you could've died—actually fucking died—or split your soul in half, ended up some sort of vengeful revenant, or—"

"Wow, gods, I had no clue severing my soul from my body on purpose was so dangerous." He throws his hand up, flinging the sardonic remark to the big top rafters. "It was the only way to terminate my contract without Yokuiv knowing. That's why I saved up all that magic to make my trailer look like a battleground, why I left part of my body behind, why we waited until the last night of a run with Phenomenae scheduled after us so Abidine could tie him up in political red tape when he refused to relocate like we knew he would—all smoke and mirrors to keep him away from Berhede until I could reincorporate and give my testimony to the Greater Circuit. But then—"

"I helped Yokuiv figure it out." It's her turn to pace, palms shoving up her forehead into her hair. "I found the tea. I told him your pendant was missing, and about the mortal who stole your record player—that was the vessel for your soul, wasn't it? And she's not a stalker, she's your liaison with Phenomenae—" She whirls. Renni, following her at a distance trying to get a word in edgewise, staggers back a startled pace. "*You* crafted those talismans."

"I'm sorry about that hex, she swears she was trying *not* to hit you."

"I wish she'd hit me with all of them." Her ears ring with Berhede's pleas, begging her to believe his innocence before being dragged away by a construct. Yokuiv could have taken him into custody at any time, but he'd wanted to make it look convincing; so he killed Enqirez and planted his arm in the illusionist's trunk with Leathan's kerchief, knowing she would look for it when she noticed it missing. Renni can't do anything now, when contacting the Circuit risks Yokuiv finding out and killing Berhede. "Maybe then I wouldn't have fucked everything up."

"You didn't." The entrance to the tent stirs and Zuna ducks inside, taking one hesitant step after another. "I did. I was supposed to take both Renni's body and the vessel the night of his 'murder,' but then Casallie showed up and I had to leave the record player behind or she'd have seen me— and I forgot to take the tea bag, realized too late to stop you going to the shop, not to mention did a piss-poor job of distracting you all yesterday."

Leathan barks out an incredulous laugh. "I *knew* you had an ulterior motive."

"Motive*s*," they correct, emphasizing the plural with a wry tilt to their maw.

Before she can ask what they mean, an incandescent wave of velvet and lightning and vanilla roils through Phenomenae like searching fingers of flame.

"Abidine," Yokuiv's voice calls in taunting sing-song. "I believe you have something of mine."

Twenty-Eight

Renni jerks as Abidine and the other Phenomenae troupers dash back inside the tent.

"Yokuiv," he croaks. Another probing wave of fury crashes over the circus. Hurt and bewilderment flood his bloodshot eyes as he glares at Leathan. "You sent for him."

"I thought they were going to kill me—I thought they'd killed *you.*" The truth, but it feels like a weak excuse. "He's looking for me, so I'll go prove I'm all right, tell him it's a misunderstanding—"

"He will kill you before giving you the opportunity." Abidine's expression, serene as steel, rivets Leathan in place. "Doubtless he sees 'rescuing' you as a chance to attack without violating the ceasefire, and bury his crimes with us for good. But this may yet prove to be in our favor."

Leathan's guilt surges sour in her gut. "I don't see how."

"We were formulating a rescue plan when you arrived, but that's no longer necessary. He's brought his hostage to us."

As if on cue, there comes a scream of agony from outside, so loud and drawn out Leathan can't tell when it ends and its echoes begin.

"Berhede—" With a stifled cry, Renni lurches towards the tent entrance. The Phenomenae ringmaster stops him with a gentle hand on his left shoulder.

"Yokuiv means to goad you out of hiding," she says, a reminder and admonishment both. "He will not hurt him too grievously. Not without you there to watch."

Berhede screams again. Renni trembles, eyes clinging to the tent's entrance, jaw tight, fist clenched. "Sure sounds pretty fucking grievous to me."

"If you want to help your lover, contact the Circuit. There's nothing to be gained by waiting now." She conjures a polished wooden cylinder sparkling with power. Glittering tassels and beads dangle from one end; on the other, Leathan glimpses engravings of flowing lihilim script before Renni clutches it to his chest with an agonized look. "Hopefully they answer the summons with some modicum of haste."

"And if they don't?"

Abidine ignores him.

"Dhov, Janecz." The aerialists, huddled shoulder to shoulder, straighten as their ringmaster addresses them. "Keep him safe until the representative arrives. Mabeqir, stay close to me, out of sight. Zuna—escort your guest beyond the threshold, and be careful. Yokuiv's constructs are prowling."

Leathan bristles, snapping her compact out of Abidine's hands when the Phenomenae ringmaster proffers it. "You want me to run?"

"He does not actually know you are here—I cloaked your compact, so he can only guess, and without full certainty one of his is behind enemy lines, he cannot enter my domain. Therefore, to avoid the utter obliteration of my outfit, yes," says Abidine, "I want you to run."

Renni and Leathan exchange one brief, terrified glance before Zuna presses a light touch to her elbow. The world dims, and something cool and soft melts over her. It's only when Renni's eyes search the spot where she's standing she realizes he can no longer see her.

"This only works if we're touching," explains Zuna, apologetic, as they lead her out of the tent. Before-her nudges, and the spy chuckles, surprised. "Well, that makes it easier."

Leathan's too full of fear to realize what she's done until she sees her fingers intertwined with theirs. If she didn't think breaking the enchantment was key to breaking her curse, she'd swear then and there to let before-her stay trapped forever. Hells, she'd fortify the web.

Zuna fetches their pendant. Leathan looks away to avoid glimpsing the bronze inside again, trying to forget they got a front and center view of *her* curse before, and trying to keep herself from whimpering every time Yokuiv sends another wave of his power searching through the circus. Searching for her.

"I swore you'd be safe if you came here." The spy tightens their grip around Leathan's hand. "I intend to keep that promise."

She wants to say she doesn't need their protection, but what comes out is, "Why did you give me the ticket?"

They consider her sidelong, mask still for once. "You know why."

We needed her on our side—

You mean you *needed her.*

The connection between them digs even deeper into her chest. She can't think around it except to state the obvious as they approach Phenomenae's threshold. "Constructs have keen senses. We should be quiet."

They pass into mortal reality and climb a steep road snaking up the hill behind Phenomenae. Suddenly Zuna shoves her behind a vending machine—Leathan struggles, but they turn her face towards the construct down the road, and she freezes. It stalks towards them, head swiveling, nose huffing.

The bones of Zuna's hips dig into the flesh of Leathan's stomach, free hand splayed flat against the wall beside her head, the strained curve of their neck filling her vision, the scent of Abidine's power strong in her nostrils as the shadows around them deepen. Her heart pounds so loud the construct must surely be able to hear.

After a long minute, the construct moves on. When the spy steps back, Leathan stumbles, knees weakened from the close call and the phantom pressure of their body on hers. She waves off the concern in their eyes and urges them around a twist in the road.

Phenomenae's big top looms below. Zuna's mask contorts—their outfit should be well behind them by now. Too late, Leathan kens a thin web of her ringmaster's power warping the world so all paths lead back here. A more sophisticated version of the trap she'd laid for the spy whose hand she now grips in a vice.

Yokuiv stands in front of Phenomenae's sole ticket booth, flanked on either side by constructs. Abidine faces him alone, her low-bridged nose a hair's width away from his. Leathan goes clammy, knowing he could force his way through the threshold at the slightest provocation.

But he doesn't look provoked. He looks how Leathan remembers him looking when he found her, all calm charm and self-assuredness, blond hair waxed into a perfect coif, clothing ironed to crisp lines. One hand is tucked into a pocket while the other glides through the disheveled curls of a man knelt beside him, bound in rope and magic both. Even knowing he'd brought Berhede, seeing the illusionist—his eyes half-lidded and downcast, shoulders hunched, blood soaking his shirt and beard and splattering the pavement beneath him—makes Leathan suck in a sharp gasp of shock.

She realizes her mistake the moment the constructs flanking Yokuiv pivot in her direction, and claps her hand over her mouth even as a third construct manifests in front of her.

It grabs her by the throat, wrenching her from Zuna's grip and the safety of the shadows. As it lifts her, she scrambles for her compact, but it snatches her wrists with two other hands and, with another, crushes her clamshell to dust. The magic inside falls to the earth like prismatic snow.

Zuna hits it with a hex; it staggers, but blasts the spy off the hillside with a burst of raw Extravaganza power. Dirt and stone vomit out in a geyser of smoke. When it clears, the spy is gone. At the bottom of the hill, Phenomenae's big top erupts into flames.

Holding her fast, the construct leaps down to the conflagration. Yokuiv stands over Abidine. The Phenomenae ringmaster struggles on hands and knees, wings wilted over her. Yokuiv toes one boot under her chin, rears his leg back, and lets fly a kick so powerful it sends the other lihilim tumbling into the trailers ten feet away. She crashes into the metal with a sickening crunch and explosion of aluminum siding, and lies still.

"Oh, my dear, sweet Leathan." Yokuiv's wolfish grin belies his mournful tone. He rolls a marble of magic through lithe fingers. It spins in slow-motion above his open palm, drawing her fascination with the sheer weight of its power. "I'm sorry I was too late to save you. Rest assured, your death—and that of every trouper Phenomenae took from me—will be avenged."

The marble careens out of his hand, streaking into a brilliant javelin of light right before piercing through the pendant prone on Leathan's chest.

TWENTY-NINE

Leathan is subsumed by a glittering sandstorm of blood and bone, shattered glass and gold. The victorious shrieks of her curse as it whips out if its prison in a frenzied miasma drowns out her screams. She's crushed back on herself, rib cage snapped wide and skin flayed open until she's nothing but a bundle of desiccated twigs and thorns wrapped around a raw, throbbing heart threaded through with shimmering tendrils of connection.

There are dozens—more than Leathan expected, more than she's ever had before—spider-silk thin and tree-trunk fat, tangled together like creeping ivy. The curse tears at them with horrible wet wrenching noises; agonizing and slow, they gouge out of her like gnarled roots clinging to the earth in a typhoon.

Casually as a cat with a ball of string, Yokuiv bats her curse away. Howling with gale-force fury, it turns its vengeance instead, to Leathan's despair, upon what's left of Phenomenae. Dhov and Janecz fight it back, while in the wreckage of the trailers Mabeqir hoists Abidine to her feet. On the far side of the blazing big top, Renni drags Berhede to safety as the curse disintegrates the constructs into mounds of ash.

Yokuiv draws Leathan's ragged form into a cradling embrace. For one delirious moment she thinks he's protecting her, until she sees the hungry glint in his crystal blue eyes, and his grin gapes open around rows and rows of sharp teeth. "Usually I prefer to wait the full century—but given the circumstances, better to harvest early than let your soul go to waste."

She thrashes weak, thorn-studded tendrils against his chest. Sharp as they are, they don't even scratch him. A horrible, burning light in the back of his throat draws her in, and in, and in. Leathan tips into his waiting maw, scrambles for something—anything—to hold on to. In her desperate flailing, she kens a flicker of power, grabs onto it for dear life, and only realizes what it is when her heart wrenches.

Her connections. They're still there, clinging on by a strained thread. Intent as she was to keep them ever forming, she'd never once reached to them for strength, fearing to strengthen them in turn and make them root into her so deeply, her curse would tear her very being apart clawing them out.

She clutches them to her now, as close as she can bear and then closer still. Power surges through them, more power than she can remember touching, but knows she's capable of handling. She reaches for before-her, too, bracing herself against the enchantment's backlash, and with her guidance weaves the power into a replica of the marble that destroyed her pendant. As Yokuiv snaps his teeth shut around her, she hurtles it straight into his mouth.

It bursts into thick tumbleweed tangles that bloom to fill the lihilim's gullet. They spill over his reddened lips, constricting around his throat and limbs faster than his power burns them away. He lets out a ragged, ethereal cry so beautiful it would make Leathan weep if she still had tear ducts, almost makes her move to help him as he struggles.

Her curse slams into her from the side, clawing and ripping and rending without a lihilim to stop it. Pain starbursts through her with each connection it tears out, and she braces to be flung away—but something snatches her free.

"I've got you," bellows the pitch-black darkness sheltering her. Zuna. They're in costume, a spindly smudge of charcoal, their mask a jagged sliver of obsidian pierced by two bloody red pits. "Hold on—*Abidine!*"

They weave protective magic as fast as her curse slashes through it, heedless of Leathan's thorns digging into their flesh, her curse biting and snapping at their back. It's overwhelming their contractual protections, shredding their costume and body into black ribbons, power effervescing off them like ash. The ground beneath them caves and cracks under the onslaught, and still they cling to her, even though they must know it's useless to fight. Leathan shrieks, wishing she could wriggle out from under them and let her curse take her. Better than being forced to watch it destroy them. She might survive her curse; she would never survive *that*.

"Don't you dare," Zuna grunts, as if they ken her thoughts. Their compact runs dry; they drop it to the bloodied earth, snap the pendant from around their neck. "You still owe me that drink, and you can throw it in my face for all I care—*Abidine where the fuck are you*—just— hold on—"

The red holes of their eyes flare. They slam their pendant into their muzzle, and chomp down with a keening growl.

As the mask's canines puncture the glass, the bronze inside liquefies, seeps out and oozes down their throat and shoulders to subsume their entire body. Zuna curls tight around Leathan, eyes wild and terrified and fixed on her, as they give one last shudder, and go still. Her thorns no longer pierce them; the curse no longer strips away flesh or magic, because there's no flesh or magic to strip away. Only cold, unyielding metal.

Yowling, her curse changes tactic, hefts them both into the air. Phenomenae magic lashes through the vortex and wraps around them, statue and tumbleweed alike, reeling them back into Renni's waiting arm. Leathan, sandwiched between him and Zuna, stares in awe at the kraken's tentacle flowing from his left shoulder, his tattoo roiling with the same kind of spellwork as Zuna's mask.

The curse tearing around them like razors is suddenly yanked away. Abidine strides towards them, one hand clenched around Leathan's writhing curse as if holding a bouquet of flowers. She motions for Renni to set Zuna and Leathan down. "To think you'd try to handle a curse this powerful on your own—"

"We were managing," says Renni, as the kraken tentacle flattens itself back into his tattoo.

With a chiding click of her tongue, Abidine melts the bronze away from the spy, siphoning it back through the holes they'd bit into their pendant. As the metal retreats, Zuna gasps in a ragged breath of air, unfurling but not relinquishing their grip around Leathan. They hack up a hunk of bronze and thrust to their ringmaster. "You took too long."

Smoothing their pendant whole, Abidine inclines her bedraggled head to another lihilim behind her, their hands tucked into their sleeves over their big belly. "Igmun insisted we ensured Yokuiv was secured in the Circuit's custody first."

"I would not believe him defeated without seeing him bound and stripped of his powers with my own eyes," they sniff. "He's slipped away from me more than once before. You cannot blame me for taking every precaution."

Abidine clicks her tongue. "Including filing all the correct forms so you could be the one sent into the field, rather than rush to our defense unsanctioned."

"How truly sorry I am to have missed all the excitement." Igmun polishes their spectacles as they survey the smoking ruins of Phenomenae. A few paces away the aerialists and Mabeqir squat around Berhede, tending to his wounds. The illusionist grits his teeth and turns away when Renni shyly tries to meet his gaze. "This will be a difficult job to salvage."

"No need. Not when I can claim the Extravaganza Eternia by right of spoils." Abidine's smile is wide and white and shining, as if this is exactly what she'd hoped would happen.

The Circuit representative lifts one eyebrow, then chuckles. "You won't look so pleased with yourself when you see how much paperwork that kind of claim entails."

"Speaking of paperwork." Abidine crouches beside Leathan, holding out a yellowed scroll of parchment cramped with flowing black script. "The gist is similar to what Yokuiv offered you, though his was a very basic boilerplate. Mine includes a few minor but significant tweaks, such as—"

Leathan doesn't wait for Abidine to explain. She hefts a tiny appendage to slap a signature of sap on the dotted line.

Her curse screams when Phenomenae magic flares up from the contract to cage it. As it shrinks into a new pendant, Leathan grows into herself again, twigs and thorns sloughing off, knitting back into skin and bones and flesh. Her rib cage barely closes over her heart before Zuna and Renni throw their arms around her, squeezing so tightly she fears she might burst—but she risks the pain to squeeze them back.

ACKNOWLEDGEMENTS

It is surreal to be writing my very first acknowledgments for my very first book—a book that would not exist without the generosity of time, support, and love from so many, including but by no means limited to:

My publisher Antonia Ward, and everyone at Ghost Orchid Press, who gave Leathan a place to call home.

My punderful editor Ed Crocker, whose—ahem—*phenomenae* enthusiasm brought me so much joy.

My cover artist and fellow Sailor Moon nerd Daniella Batsheva, who created the mahou shoujo AF cover of my wildest dreams.

Everyone at Writing the Other, whose font of workshops and resources have helped and continue to help me elevate my craft.

Everyone in my online writing communities, especially B'Write Moon, Scriveners Local 23, and the SFWA weekly writing dates, who make me feel connected from so far away.

My first readers GJ, Ruby, Dianne, Annie, Rebecca, and most especially Jessa, CJ Lavigne, Clara Kumagai, and Daniel Meyer, whose invaluable feedback, and far more importantly, friendship, I would be lost to the cursed winds without.

My husband Jeff, who held me once on top of a mountain to protect me from the cold and snow and has never stopped holding me since. I love you so much.

My cats Kurama and Hiei, who are curled up napping in my lap as I type, making sure I stay on task as always.

All my friends, family, teachers, and mentors who have encouraged, nurtured, and nourished me into the person and writer I am, and will be.

There aren't words enough to describe the sheer amount of gratitude I have for every one of you who, in too many ways to list or count, helped me bring this story out of my head into the world. Thank you, thank you; with all my heart and soul, a million times and a million more—thank you.

Kristin Osani
April 2024

ABOUT THE AUTHOR

Kristin Osani (she/her) is a queer fantasy writer who lives with her husband in northeastern Japan, where she works as a Japanese-to-English video game translator and manga editor when she's not writing, working on nerdy cross-stitching, or cuddling her two cats.

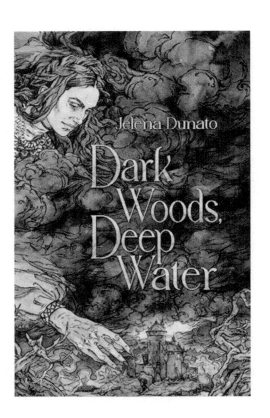

Jelena Dunato

Dark
Woods,
Deep
Water

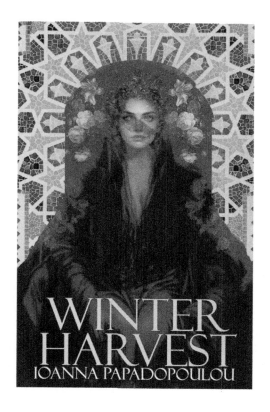

FIND ALL OUR TITLES AT

GHOSTORCHIDPRESS.COM

Printed in Great Britain
by Amazon